FRAGMENTS

(Töredékek)

Kiára Árgenta

OPENING CHAPTER

Copyright © Kiára Árgenta 2015

All rights reserved. This book or any portion thereof may not be reproduced or used in any manner whatsoever without the express written permission of the publisher except for the use of brief quotations in a book review.

First Printing, 2015

ISBN 10: 1-904958-55-9

ISBN 13: 9781904958550

published by

*Opening Chapter
Cardiff, Wales*

www.openingchapter.com

I write this for you.
Always.
K

Kiára Árgenta

Kiára Árgenta grew up in Paris before moving to Wales where she studied Russian at university. She worked as a journalist before leaving to live in Spain and then Hungary. She currently lives in Budapest and is a full-time writer.

*Fragments is a sequel to Infinity
but can be read as its own story*

LILLA

Budapest is beautiful. The first week I arrived here after living for so many years in southern Hungary I felt the depression rise from my skull so I could admire the handsome buildings and just walk along anonymously. In the south, I had a fear of meeting anyone who would ask how I was. I always felt terrible so I could not bear to be asked. The love of my life is dead. There are no words capable of describing how I feel.

I wish I could paint like Picasso and display my emotion in intense colour and pain. I moved into my new apartment in the green II district with my daughter, Natalija, who was only two years old and it was a bright February day and sun shone through the skylights. This entrancing trick of cold sunlight made me think that maybe, just maybe I could shake off the greyness which had settled behind my eyes for so long rendering the world monochrome. The first objects I placed in this lovely apartment were Kiára's photos and I hung them in every single room obsessively. She is always here with me. I do not care what people say about how long you should grieve for and this is not such a good idea to have so many pictures of your pain in the living space. It is my choice to hang on to my sadness and I do not follow rules. Ever.

As I was feeling better after the change of location, I kept getting approached by women everywhere; usually foreign and beautiful but I just couldn't face dating anyone. I didn't want to touch them, kiss them, be near them or even have dinner with them despite their good looks. I stare at myself in the mirror wanting to see what they see. I see my jet black curls, dark eyes, handsome face and toned body; I see that I am István the first king of Hungary. I am sure of this. I am immortal.

But my Queen is dead. She was the only one who understood I was a reincarnation of István a Király from the year 1000. I told her I waited 1000 years for her and she never laughed or thought I was crazy. She believed me. My shrink tells me I am having delusions but I cannot listen to him. Then at other times I forget the centuries of blood which runs through my dark veins and I am hurled into a depression so deep I cannot climb out. I am trying to look after Natalija but I am not feeling well. She is so young and her mother is forgotten by her apart from when she points to the photos. She knows her image but not her personality. I have been so heartbroken after Kiára's death that once or twice I have sealed myself in my car in the garage with the keys on the ignition but the face of Natalija does not leave my mind and I know I cannot do it. Natalija; my precious little girl.

And then the guilt bites. *I am a selfish man, how can I even contemplate leaving this girl alone?*

I cannot do this to her. I never walk near the Duna River especially the Szabadság Híd where Kiára attempted suicide that March day when I was abroad. I am afraid I will not resist the pull of the dark water and in a split second I could be over the bridge and my little girl will be alone. On my saddest days, I cannot look at the Duna unless I view it at night when the parliament and the castle are glowing gold with lights through the blackness. These beautiful lights give the illusion of a softer fairytale world, yet in the morning they are gone and everything is grey again.

Despite the change of location a year ago, I still cannot move on. There is no beginning or end to the grieving process. It stretches into infinity. Because I waited a lifetime for my love, the only hope of recovery is her reincarnation. I have to chase this dream of finding the ghost of my long lost Queen in someone else even if it explodes like a volcano in my face, and I am left picking up the fragments of my already damaged heart. I have been searching for her likeness everywhere but I do not find it. I look obsessively for Kiára all over Budapest and when I travel abroad for dental conferences, I scan airports, hotels, everywhere but she is not there. Occasionally I see her from a distance, my Kiára, but when I get closer it is not her. Sometimes I see the same hair or the same smile in a woman, but never the whole image. My shrink tells me I just need to go through the bereavement process; it is not healthy to try to look for her in someone else. I will end up with a woman who can never live up to her. He is wrong. I need to find her beauty and soul in someone else. I am obsessing about it every day. I take my medication religiously now as I have finally acknowledged that I am sick with bipolar disorder and that I have been sick for a long time but I do not listen to the shrink's advice about everything. I am a doctor too and I know what is best for me. I know that to find the image of Kiára in another woman will save me.

I just know.

I am working in a new dental surgery near my apartment in Budapest, having sold my own dental practice in the south. I wanted to be part of a bigger team so I could be anonymous. I take on more surgical cases than I did before, specialising in oral-maxillal facial surgery. I find the surgery takes my mind off the pain which is still as raw as yesterday and the day before yesterday and all my yesterdays stretching back in a horrible straggly cord to that day in April when I woke up next to the lifeless love of my life. She had survived her suicide attempt but her heart was damaged from the two cardiac arrests she suffered after jumping into the icy water. I didn't know. I thought she had survived her suicide and although she needed tablets for her heart afterwards, I never considered that it would fail on her, on us. I thought she would be with me forever.

I had the best year of my life with her before she slipped away from me for good.

It is January when I see her, almost a year after I arrived in Budapest. I have been driving the streets of the downtown every week and scanning all the faces in the crowd but so far I have not found my Kiára. But this afternoon I am not searching, so the girl in front of me is so unexpected. It jolts me with a strange electricity which shoots through my body like a magical current. She is around 20 years old; hauntingly beautiful and so like Kiára as she passes me on the street, just one frosty obsessive and possessive breath away. She is looking down at the dusting of snow on the pavement so she does not see me. She is wearing a white winter coat and glittery silver hair slides and this adds to the feeling of her purity; Kiára's angel descended from Heaven to reach me. I have to follow her, I have to. I have to talk to her. I am holding Natalija as I walk through a sugar coating of snow near my apartment. This white powder which covers everything makes the moment more magical as today the world is beautiful, if only for today. Tomorrow I might feel like Hell again. As the sun splits through the evergreen trees low and fragile, I know this is my moment and I have to seize it or it will be lost forever and I will always wonder what might have been.

I turn quickly as she passes and call, "Excuse me, do I know you? Do you come to our dental surgery? I think I have seen you there. Eszter isn't it?" I give her a radiant smile as if I am sure of this. I know it isn't and I have never seen her before but I have to come up with some credible reason to talk to her.

She looks directly at me with those dark eyes so familiar, so beautiful with their jet black lashes, they burn right into my soul; she has come back to me, my Kiára but there is no flicker of recognition there for her. She looks at me like a stranger which I am.

I feel stupid and say, "I am sorry, you look like someone, I made a mistake." My heart is sinking. She will turn away and walk on now and the delicate moment will be lost forever.

She is Kiára to me, until she speaks shyly and delicately without the confidence of Kiára and her voice makes me picture ice crystals and snowflakes falling. It is a beautiful sound and it adds to the feeling of her not being real; an ice princess. She tells me politely *she doesn't know me, but she has seen me going into my apartment once before. She doesn't live in the II district but she has been to visit her dentist. However, it is not the surgery I work in.*

Yes, of course I know this myself.

She wishes she lived around here. "It is so pretty," she says looking at the evergreen trees around us with their dusting of snow. "I live in the XIV district with my mother. It is not nice where we live; dark streets and no green spaces."

I tell her *I am a dentist and surgeon, maybe she would like to see our practice sometime? We are based near here.*

"No," she says fearful. "I am afraid of the dentist."

"Please don't be afraid of me," I say. I give her a beautiful smile.

She laughs as she thinks it is a joke. I am serious. If she knew me she would be afraid.

I see her teeth are very straight and white. Naturally straight, she has not needed orthodontics. Her mouth is lovely. I want to kiss that mouth.

Natalija is restless in my arms and reaches for the girl's long hair which is wavy and dark like Kiára's.

She looks so like Kiára I am lost in this girl's beauty. Have I dreamed her up? Maybe she will disappear just like she appeared in front of me.

"What a lovely little daughter you have, can I hold her?" says the girl. "She is beautiful. She could be a model. She looks like you with her pretty spirals of black hair and dark eyes."

I hand over Natalija who is happy to be given attention. Maybe because I am with Natalija it makes me braver. I ask tentatively would the girl like a coffee before she goes home as we are right outside my apartment. "Right here," I say pointing up at the balcony. She looks up and sees the pretty balcony with its twisted iron railings and it looks inviting from outside. I know Natalija is helping me gain her trust. An older man with a child is someone to be trusted. An older man alone is someone she should not trust.

She hesitates for a split moment and I know her instincts are telling her not to, but she looks at me in my designer suit; immaculate and handsome. She looks at her watch and I am afraid she will say no and this beautiful moment will be lost forever.

I can give her a ride home, no trouble, I add.

I am so happy lost in this moment I am smiling despite the rejection she will probably give me. Usually, I cannot smile these days.

She looks at Natalija and this is the deciding factor. A man with a beautiful little girl is not going to hurt her. "Sure, that's sweet," she says. "My name is Lilla." She follows me obediently, still holding Natalija.

She is too innocent. She should not be going into strange men's apartments. I could be anyone; she doesn't know for sure I am a dentist and surgeon. I could be a sadistic man wanting to imprison her and hurt her. I do want to imprison her and never let her go but I would never do that. But I can slowly trap her if I can manage to tie her up with silken cords of love and keep her forever. The fact she seems so young makes me feel over-protective already. As though I want to take her and shield her from all the bad and horror in this world and keep her safe. I want to climb into bed with this girl and never let her go; inhale her sweet golden skin and love her. If she knew what I was thinking she would be running away screaming by now; that I am already picturing her in my bed as I inhale her hair, her skin in order to breathe life back into my dead soul would scare the Hell out of anyone.

I take her coat off and see her hair is longer than Kiára's but with the same gentle wave and dark shade of brown. Those beautiful mesmerising eyes and face are identical, just slightly younger as if I have met Kiára as she was at 20 and not 30. I assess her height as she removes her shoes and she is a couple of centimetres shorter, but with the slim doll-like fragility of my lost love. I am staring at her helplessly and she looks embarrassed, as if she is now realising this is not a good idea. She will think I am strange so I quickly start gabbling about the coffee. "Come and see what type you would like," I tell her. "All sorts, I have everything here, home-made cake if you like."

I am very shy. Gone are the days when I could charm any woman if I wanted. I have not approached any since Kiára died although they have approached me but I do not care for them. I am shaking with nerves as I make the coffee and I tip in way too much and the coffee will make me shake as well once we drink it. I was told by my shrink to avoid coffee with my bipolar depression, it can be a trigger but the meds they give me are so strong I am so spaced out in the morning and I need to be sharp for my work. This angel Lilla sits on my sofa with her coffee and I do not know what to do. I place some small cakes on the table and tell her, "home-made from the finest chocolate". She reaches for one.

I have brought this ice princess into my house and I am grateful that Natalija is plying her with toys and books, demanding her attention because I do not know what to say. I just stare at her transfixed by her beauty. She talks about school in between admiring Natalija's dolls. I suddenly feel out of my depth. School; she is just a child. She could be Natalija's older sister.

I can't date a child, can I? God, how old is she? 15, 16, 17, but she looks older. Maybe we can just be friends and she can play with Natalija until she has matured ready for me. She said my daughter was adorable, she could be the babysitter then I would get to see her all the time and just wait until she was old enough before I make any moves. I have an au pair, Kata but I could ask Natalija to help out as Kata is doing a lot for me right now.

Yes, that could work; she can see Natalija then, it is a good excuse. She must have a boyfriend anyway, a lovely girl like her is soon going to mention her sweetheart who is going to be the same age as her and my hope, my newly-formed dreams are going to die and turn to ashes with that sentence.

She is 17, younger than the age I first guessed when I saw her on the street and this makes me more nervous but old enough to be legal. I suddenly want to do bad things to her. I picture her in my bed in red and black silk underwear while I tie her wrists to the bedframe while the candles flicker and burn. Then I feel guilt. The poor girl thinks I am a gentleman not an animal. I am 45 and I am just staring at her lost for words. I have been existing in a dull, damp fog and here is my beautiful light in the darkness. Moving to Budapest a year ago worked for a week in that it helped to heal some of my heart but it did nothing to lift the mist from my eyes. I am sad all the time since Kiára's death. I don't work the long hours I did before. I hate missing out on seeing Natalija and in my new dental practice, I tell my colleagues nothing about my life and I work two-thirds of what I did before. I could no longer carry on with the 12 hour days I did when I was the principal dentist in my own surgery in the south when I was splitting my time between the dentistry and oral-maxillal facial surgery at the hospital. Especially as my illness worsened since then and the doctors advised me for my own health I had to cut down, or I would keep ending up in hospital in a manic episode and it could result in me having to give up work entirely if I didn't listen to what they told me.

I try my best; if only for Natalija I must keep going.

And right now the mist has lifted and I have a shred of hope I am clinging on to desperately. I must be careful not to ruin it. She is just a girl, this angel Lilla. My mother was called Lilla. It is one of my favourite names.

Lilla looks around the living room. "What a beautiful apartment you have," she says in awe.

I ask her would she like to see all the rooms and she obediently pads around the three-bedroomed apartment admiring everything although she says the master bedroom looks very dark with black walls and deep purple bedcovers. Even the ensuite bathroom has black walls but there are a lot of mirrors and plants. I watch her and think *she doesn't know I am dark, very dark. My soul is the colour of burnt wood; charred and dead.* She sees the photos of Kiára and walks over to one.

"She's lovely," she says more to the photo than me. "Is this your girlfriend? Is she a model or an actress?"

"No," I tell her. "She was my wife. She died nearly 2 years ago, although she did some modelling for magazines once."

"I'm sorry," says Lilla. She looks at the photo then at me again. "She looks a lot like me. That could almost be me in ten years."

"Yes," I say. "She looks just like you." *Just like you*, hangs in the air and surrounds her in a bubble. Lilla looks at me and a flicker of recognition ghosts across her face. *Just like you*.

I am afraid she will leave now because she will know she is here because of her resemblance to the only girl I ever loved. She is still calling me, Ö*n*, the formal address instead of *te*. I tell her to use *te*.

She doesn't say she is leaving after this, she still seems relaxed in my apartment and I want her to stay forever. She sits down on the bed. "I don't know how people do it, fall in love. I have never even dated a boy," she says this in a dreamy innocent way and there she is sitting on my bed.

"You are too beautiful for them, they must be afraid of you, afraid of rejection," I tell her stepping closer. "You are so beautiful, Lilla. Like a movie star." I stare into her eyes unblinking and then I look down as I feel stupid. I have let my feelings show and I do not feel comfortable doing this. Although by the way she looks at me and then looks away, I know she finds me attractive. She is shy too. I sit on the bed but not too near her. I do not want to scare her.

In the other room, I hear Natalija talking to her dolls still lost in her toys on the sofa.

I gaze at Lilla as she sits next to me. She looks at me with those beautiful eyes and I am smouldering inside. I can smell her perfume. It is too sweet, too childish, like cheap candy and she has those tacky false nails decorated with jewels which I hate and a frosty pink lipstick. If she was with me I would buy her an expensive scent, like Coco Chanel and paint her nails a pale delicate pink and those lovely lips fiery red. She is going to tell me to go to Hell; I am too old for her. I am a dirty older man trying to pick up a young girl.

I have ruined my moment.

Then she is in my arms and her kisses are spun-sugar sweet, her delicate mouth inexperienced. Too sweet, too child-like and yet too lasting. Her lipstick tastes like candy. She gently runs her hands through my hair and those delicate cool fingers are touching my face. My heart is racing. I hold her for a long time. I am afraid of what I want to do taking over if I kiss her much more. Then she will run away, this girl who has never even been kissed. I gently caress her hair and kiss her.

My love, I want you right now, I think.

Especially as we are sitting on my bed of all places. This is just too dangerous.

I worry she is doing this as a test, just to see if she likes to kiss a boy or man. She will not be doing it because she likes me. It is an experiment and then she can go out into the world and start her dating.

"I like the way you kiss," she says. "Your mouth is very sweet and clean. I guess a dentist would be clean. You are so handsome. I never saw such a handsome man."

I don't know if she means all this but it is nice. But I know she is right about my mouth.

I smile at her and smooth the waves of her hair back and tell her *she is the most beautiful girl I have ever seen. The exact image of my dead love.* I do not add the last part. It sounds sinister.

I tentatively ask her to visit again stressing that Natalija would love to see her, she can babysit if she would like, if she has time and I will pay her well. I offer a high rate just be sure she will come back.

"Sure, I would like that," she smiles. "But I also like you too," she adds shyly.

My heart is about to explode through my chest. *She likes me and wants to see me again.*

"You are such a lovely girl, Lilla. I really want to see you soon," I say. I kiss her hand making her laugh and I take that beautiful hand and lead her back to the living room or I am going to lose all control and leap on her if we sit in my bedroom much longer and that will be it. End of story.

Lilla visits me a lot after this, she babysits after school some evenings and on weekend days. We talk about nothing in particular and once Natalija is put to sleep, I kiss her and hold her and tell her *she is so beautiful, the most beautiful girl in the world.* On her second visit I am so afraid she will not arrive that I am sick with nerves. But she does and I present her with a bottle of Coco Chanel. She sprays on way too much in delight, not used to heavy expensive scents and I close my eyes and I am back in the room with Kiára who wore Coco Chanel all the time. I always drive Lilla home afterwards and she says *she hasn't even been in a car other than a taxi, my car is so luxurious.* Once I return to the apartment I inhale the perfume which is in the air, on the sofa and her spirit remains; or Kiára's spirit like some wonderful sweet ghost.

The difference between our experiences is like a jagged mountain range but for now it seems trouble-free. I can show Lilla what she has never experienced and she has a childish wonder for the world which makes me happy when I see her face light up.

But she is intelligent despite her innocence. She speaks good English and French and a little Spanish and Italian and tells me she will study languages and literature at university in the autumn. She teaches Natalija English by reading her books as I am keen for her to be bilingual at least and the sooner she starts the better. I have tried English with Natalija but I end up speaking to her in Hungarian mainly as I am not patient enough when I am depressed. I need to speak my own tongue.

I ask Lilla can she stay one weekend at the end of January and this has moved us to the next level. It is not a girly sleepover. I do not know what she thinks we will do but she will be in my bed from Friday until Sunday. I do not tell her this. I wonder if she is expecting to curl up next to Natalija in her pajamas after reading *The Snow Queen* in English. This is as far from what I want as it gets.

I am planning to gently seduce her and hope I don't scare her away forever. I hope if I give her some wine and tell her that she is the loveliest angel to come down to earth I can have her in my bed.

She must know in her heart that she looks so much like my dead love, Kiára. There are photos of her in every single room. But we do not talk about this, as it was mentioned on her first visit.

She agrees to stay over and says she has to pretend to her mother she is with a friend but she is happy enough. I take her to a magnificent restaurant on the Friday night and I have given her a lovely black dress and some gold shoes to wear and she is full of childish delight at her gifts. I thought about the red and black silk underwear I had also bought for her but changed my mind and left it in the wardrobe. She will know I am after sex and she might change her mind about staying this weekend. Of course I am after sex but I have to be careful with this totally inexperienced girl. I could hurt her and she might never come back.

Lilla doesn't mind at all that Natalija is with us. The scent of Coco Chanel hangs heavy in the air and it evokes the spirit of Kiára. In the flickering romantic candlelight of the restaurant, I am with Kiára as Lilla appears much older when she is dressed up and with make up on. I think of the one date I had three months ago with a beautiful American woman who had brashly asked me out and then complained and whined, 'Why do you have to bring your daughter everywhere?' and sulked throughout the dinner. I couldn't bear to see her again and tipped her out by her apartment and drove away as fast as I could. I couldn't even kiss her goodnight. Lilla accepts Natalija as part of my life; I explain I work a lot and I want to see as much of Natalija as possible but Lilla tells me *there is no need to apologise, she loves seeing the little girl.* I give Lilla a glass of wine and she loosens up, loses her shyness. She is so lovely. I call her Kiára by mistake and I am mortified but she laughs and says *really it's okay. She is flattered. Kiára was so beautiful. How old was she when she died?*

"34," I say. And I feel sad the instant I say it.

Lilla reaches for my hand and tells me *she thinks she understands this love feeling.* I take that as a sign. She holds my hand across the table and I know I have found what I have been searching for.

When I take her home I think she is too pure, how am I going to get her into my bed? I have seen her pajamas in her weekend bag and I feel guilty. They are so pink, so childish and her underwear is so girly. Even her toothbrush box is a frosted glittery pink. I just want to keep her that way, like untouched snowflakes and just as delicate. My ice queen. I don't want to break her, she is as delicate as crystal.

She is shy again after she has read Natalija a bedtime story and asks *where is she going to sleep? In the spare room?*

"Here, with me. You can read me a bedtime story too if you like. But we can just sleep, Lilla. I promise I won't do anything; I would just love to sleep next to you," I say. I get out a book and place it on the bed but in my mind I am doing everything to her, throwing the bedtime story book across the room and ravishing her beautiful flesh. To keep up the innocent act, I even change into pajamas which I never wear unless I am sick. Just so it looks like I am going to curl up and go to sleep.

"Okay," she says happily without hesitation but I see her staring at me as I am getting changed, looking at my toned body. She has probably never seen a man undress in her life. She stares at me for too long and then goes into the bathroom and cleans her teeth.

I gently remove the black dress I bought for her to go out when she returns back to my candlelit bedroom and kiss her shoulders and in this trick light as in the restaurant, I see only Kiára. My dead love reincarnated in this beautiful angel. I place her on the bed gently and keep telling my mind to treat her as fragile, she is just a girl. "Do you want your pajamas?" I ask reaching for them. She takes my arm and stops me, "No, I don't need them, do I?"

I lean over her and kiss her and she starts to unbutton my pajama top. She knows what she is doing or more like she knows what I want to do to her. "You smell so nice, István. You are the most handsome man I have ever seen. Are you going to love me now?" she says as she inhales my neck. God, I am drowning. I hope I don't hurt her. I tell her she is an angel come down to earth to be with me. She laughs. I mean it. She doesn't think I do.

That night I believe I am with Kiára but I am keeping in my mind that this is young Kiára. *You are not an animal*, I tell myself. *She asked you to love her, not fuck her violently.* When we sleep afterwards, I dream of her. The heavy aroma of Coco Chanel fills the room and makes me dizzy. I think I am in love.

I wake up and stare at the ceiling and Kiára is lying next to me, her warm body wrapped around me. She is younger, much younger and I wonder what happened, did I travel back in time? What happened?

I am afraid as it takes me back to the worst morning of my life when I woke up next to Kiára and she was at peace in her sleep but there was no breath and no pulse and she had had a cardiac arrest only a year after her suicide attempt. Her heart had been damaged and had just failed sometime in that grey hour before morning.

I am startled now and I sit up in fear, desperately feeling for her pulse and then I know; I am with Lilla. Kiára's image. She is real, she is breathing. But I am afraid she will open her eyes and regret everything and leave my apartment and me and my torn heart. *She wanted me*, she said last night. *She wanted me to*.

"I love you," I had said into her hair as I stroked her face. But I can only see Kiára. I know what I love is Kiára and if this girl was not the image of her, I wouldn't love. I don't love Lilla, I love what she represents. But I want Lilla. I want Lilla so much I never want her to leave. She has none of the fire smouldering within; the volcanic anger and intense passion of Kiára. She is sweet and gentle and young and I am afraid of hurting her in bed.

Natalija is shouting through the door to let her in. I have locked it and she is distressed outside. It doesn't wake Lilla as I get up to open the door.

"Kiára?" says Natalija puzzled as she sees the figure in the bed. "Has mama come home?" She climbs onto the bed and on top of Lilla. "Mama?" Her jet spirals of hair brush over Lilla's face as she looks closer. Lilla opens her eyes.

"Mama? Is that you?" asks Natalija not sure at all. She can only remember Kiára through the photos in the apartment. Lilla smiles, "No, it's Lilla." She sits up in bed.

"You are in István's bed," says Natalija, her dark eyes confused and unsure."Why?"

"She was tired," I tell her. "She needed to sleep."

"Okay," says Natalija. She does not understand why this isn't Kiára.

"Go and sit in the kitchen, baby girl. Lilla will want to make you breakfast now," I tell her.

I gather up the sheets when Lilla is in the bathroom. I must have hurt her last night although I held my full passion back and didn't let myself go. I wanted to devour her, bite her delicate skin and taste her sweet blood. The evidence I stole this girl's purity is on the sheets and I feel guilt and I have to throw it all in the wash before the cleaner arrives. The cleaner will think I am a terrible man taking advantage of this beautiful innocent girl. I feel bad. She will judge me. I am always feeling guilty about everything these days, after Kiára's death. Lilla's pink pajamas lie untouched by the side of the bed and I feel even more guilt. I seduced this girl who did expect some kind of sleepover with a movie and popcorn not a lusty older man who only wanted her in his bed.

Lilla has never asked my age. I still don't know what she really thinks of me. She is quiet and sweet but I know she could smash my heart to pieces with her youthful indifference. There is a carelessness about her despite her sweetness as if she would just get up and leave without a second thought. Or it is a feeling she is not of this world because of her beauty, her delicate body, that dreamy look in her eyes. Because of this I want to possess her there and then. I want to own this Lilla; my prize.

She comes to the breakfast table her eyes clear and lovely. "I feel different," she says. "I'm not a girl any longer." She looks thoughtful, and I don't know if this makes it good or bad or indifferent.

Did she like the night or was it all the same to her? I don't know. She doesn't seem to display feelings, whether good or bad. She is serene. An ice princess.

"Mama," says Natalija reaching out her arms. I don't know if Natalija just wants to call her this or if she half believes Kiára has returned. Lilla lifts her from her seat and sits her on her knees.

I know right then for Natalija and for me I need Lilla. I need her like a drug. And I need her to be Natalija's mother.

I'm sorry I stole your purity, my angel. My sweet girl.

When the cleaner arrives I feel I have to keep telling her Lilla is teaching Natalija English, she is here this weekend as she has a break from her studies.

The cleaner just laughs and says, "Is that why you changed your own sheets? I only put fresh ones on 2 days ago."

I am so ashamed I can't say a word.

I hear the cleaner laughing as she hoovers the apartment.

I bake Lilla the best Chinese I can that evening; I want to show her I can cook and Chinese was one of Kiára's favourites. I let her put Natalija to bed as I light the candles on the table. I want everything perfect for her. I want her to stay forever.

"How kind of you to make all this for me," she says. In the candlelight I am aware I call her Kiára once or twice and the evening has a strange dreamlike quality as though I am drunk. We are drinking green tea although I said we could have champagne if she wanted but green tea is best.

Later in the bedroom, I see she has packed her pajamas away, thank God. I kiss her and in the passion of the moment I tell her I love her. Anyone would know that it is pure lust not love; she is so beautiful. I know that but I think I love her as she is my reincarnation, as though I created this angel of my lost love. I wanted to find her so desperately and I did.

Right outside my apartment.

As she is falling asleep in my arms, I ask her *did she take her pill.*

"Which one?" she asks me sleepily with her hands in my hair.

"The contraceptive pill," I tell her.

"No, I don't have any," she says. She is so naive and innocent she seems about 14. I am not worried. I already have it all planned out and if my beautiful princess gives me my heir to the throne too soon, then it isn't soon enough. I want another reason to keep her in the amber palace I am building for her but I tell her *I will get her the pill as I am a doctor otherwise she will have to pay for it on prescription.*

She then worries, "Should I have taken it, István? Will it be okay?"

I honestly don't know about that, you lovely angel. Your innocence is so sweet.

But I tell her *everything will be perfect, please don't worry. I will get her the pill for next time she is here.*

"Okay," she says happily settling into my chest.

She should worry. She should worry a lot if she knew anything about me.

ADDICTION

It is only February, right before my birthday and I have moved Lilla from my bed into my whole life. I tell her I want her to stay with me in my apartment. I need her every night, every morning.

She says *she will move in with me. She would be really happy to do that.*

"Am I your girlfriend?" she has already asked after our first weekend together with childish delight.

"You are much more than that, Lilla. You are my Queen," I told her as I kissed her hand.

She likes this as it is all so new to her. So for her to move in with me is not going too fast for this naive young girl. I have only known her a month.

In truth, I just cannot live without her. I am a junkie and I need my fix of her morning and night. I realise it is pure obsession and physical lust and driven mainly by the fact she is so like my lost love. At night I actually believe it is my Queen I am with. I inhale the deep scent of Coco Chanel and I am travelling back in time to meet the flesh of Kiára, my darling. I do not see this as unhealthy. I do not see this is not going to end happily for either of us. I just do not want to see this. I am in the moment. I am lost.

But it is a wonderful feeling after the years of loneliness when I vowed never to be with another woman. In this dizzy vortex of addiction, I actually believe I am in love with Lilla. I waited 6 months before I took Kiára to my bedroom and I have taken Lilla there after only 2 weeks. Time is accelerating as I get older. There is no time to wait these days.

I have to keep telling Kiára as I talk to all the photographs in the apartment why I am doing this. *'My love, you came back in the body of another girl. I am not cheating on you, I promise. It is you I love, Lilla is the image of you. Give me a sign, a sign that she is you.'*

I am convinced at times she has descended from Heaven and is now existing in the flesh of this lovely girl. I do not see this is distorted thinking. I am thinking I have found my Queen again.

No, I am so convinced of this. She came back to me, but she hasn't told me yet; I am still waiting for a sign.

I wait outside Lilla's mother's apartment in my car in a dark street in the XIV district. This is no place for my princess to be. I want her in an amber palace, dressed in white with diamonds in her hair, this lovely girl as delicate as crystal. Natalija asks from the back seat *is mama staying for good this time?*

Yes, I tell her. *She is.*

Forever.

Lilla leaves carrying her suitcases followed by her mother who is shouting. I get out to help Lilla with her bags. When her mother sees me she turns her venom on me. "You sick, sick man. You must be 20 years older than her and you have brainwashed her into living with you. I can't do anything to change her mind. You better be giving her the contraceptive pill because I am not paying for it," she says. I see with disgust she has a cigarette in her hand. She is nothing like Lilla, she bears no resemblance to my darling whatsoever.

I don't tell her it is a bigger age gap than that. I just tell her that *she doesn't need to worry, I am a doctor so of course I get her the pills.*

Lilla holds up her arms and says, "Anya, please. I love him. He is a good man. He is a dentist and surgeon. He is kind. He has a lovely little girl. Please be happy for me. He is taking care of me."

Her mother turns away and says, "Just go, he will take everything from you. Just don't end up with a baby at your age, your whole life ahead of you and university and you run off with this man. He will throw you aside and you will end up a single mother in some horrible apartment with no future. Well ruin your life then, I give up with you." She is still ranting as she punches the numbers into the apartment block entry pad.

Lilla does love me then, or has just said she loves me. I am very happy about that.

But she is wrong. I am not a good man and I will take everything from her. I want to possess her body and her soul. I want her to be mine forever. I don't want another man to touch her.

She will never run away from me then.

Everything is racing in my head and I want more and more and more, faster and faster.

I will not wait.

I tell her how wrong her mother is. I never would throw her aside. I want her with me forever.

"Do you love me? I don't want to end up a single mother in a horrible apartment. So is it love?" asks Lilla.

"I love you enough to reshape the moon for you, baby," I say and squeeze her hand.

Everything I am feeling is so intense at times I actually think I could reshape the moon. I feel so powerful.

I hang her clothes in the wardrobe and I notice how cheap they are. I will buy her expensive dresses and shoes, everything she wants. I will give her so much she will never ever want to leave. I will put her in that amber palace.

I am in Heaven now, but there is an anxious feeling gnawing away at the back of my skull. I have Lilla here but she is not fully mine yet. She could just leave at any time. Nothing is keeping her here apart from the way I treat her. *If I break the crystal, I could still lose her forever.*

I tell Lilla *I haven't been honest with her, I am*

sorry.

"How?" she asks me. It is my birthday and she has made me a cake with Natalija decorated by the number 36 in chocolate sprinkles. Natalija is busy icing around the edges trying to write **István**. The cake is a mess; sticky, sickly chocolate despite the quality ingredients I gave them to use as I hate junk food.

I am older than 36. She guessed 36 before and I never corrected her.

"I am 46. I am 46 years old," I say.

"46 years old," repeats Natalija and laughs as she adds some magic candles to the cake. "Magic candles," she says happily. "You never get old, you never die." She is talking to the cake and doesn't notice the tension between me and Lilla.

Lilla displays the only hurt betrayal I have seen in her so far. She just looks at me as if I told her something really awful. I didn't lie, I just didn't make a big deal of my age and she could have looked at my passport after all. It was in the drawer next to the bed.

"What else are you hiding, István? Are you married? Are you really a surgeon and dentist or did you lie about that too?" she looks at me more with sadness than anything else.

"I am sorry. And I am what I say I am. I never lied about my wife; she died. You are my first since her and I want you to be my last. I have hardly even dated women. But I am sick too. I have bipolar disorder."

"What does that mean? What happens to you?" she says. She is looking afraid now as if I said I turn into a vampire every night.

Which I do, or more like I did before but I haven't let myself with my delicate Lilla yet. She will be running straight back to her mother if I start biting her beautiful flesh and sucking on her sweet blood.

"I have always had it but it means I get very depressed and then extremely happy but I take medication for it. It is more like how the seasons change, you know when you feel sadder in winter and summer is so great. You don't need to worry," I tell her.

This is the biggest understatement of bipolar I could imagine; she should worry if she knows anything about bipolar one, the more serious end of the spectrum but I am afraid she will leave if she knows how bad my illness can be.

She sighs and tells me *the age gap is not so bad. I don't look my age and what can she do now anyway.*

"I'm already in love with you. I can't do anything but I wish you had told me. You are older than my father would be," she says with sadness.

I know I am not being honest. She hasn't seen how terrible my bipolar gets, how it has worsened after Kiára's death despite medication and the only reason I held myself together and what stopped me ending up in hospital was the fear I would lose Natalija. If she was taken away, I might never get her back. I have no relatives alive to look after her and Kiára's mother died soon after her. She also fell apart after her death.

"What happened to your father?" I ask as it is the first time she has mentioned him. I guessed her parents were divorced. But it sounds like he died since she said 'would be'.

Lilla doesn't answer but I can see she does not like my question and she picks up the cake. I think she is going to throw it at me. Then she puts it down and asks Natalija to change the 3 to a 4. Her anger seems to melt but she has not answered my question about her father so I don't push it. Maybe he is dead or maybe he was cruel to her or he walked out on them. Either way she does not want to talk about it. Her mother has also has not been cruel but not been particularly good to her and Lilla clearly does not want to talk about her family.

She smiles at me with her beautiful and angelic expression showing me everything is okay again and I think I have found what I thought I could never find. "I love you, Lilla," I say. The words are empty and they feel empty. They are totally devoid of feeling. Trees stripped of leaves, just bare and plain. Those words stick to my tongue like that sickly cake will. I hate cake. I will only eat some to please Natalija. I will take the rest into work and give it away.

I have been gentle with Lilla, handling her like a doll. Unlike the smouldering passion I shared with Kiára, I am afraid of scaring this inexperienced girl, so I have been careful when I have been dying to let go. I want to bite her and suck her blood. I want to be rough and pin her against the shower wall but I am afraid. She is delicate and innocent and I can't. I take out the red and black silky underwear I bought for her but it doesn't turn her from a sweet girl into the passionate lover I want and need. I was hoping it would. She is hesitant and as I look at her lying there she looks as though she could be a model in a magazine; stunningly beautiful but not real life flesh and blood. She is still very inhibited in bed.

One night I bite her shoulder hard and taste her sweet blood and she screams and pulls my hair and tells me to stop. I can't and she digs her nails in my back and scratches me and shouts, "Stop it, István. You're really hurting me." The sensation of her nails on my skin whips me back to Kiára and the unrestrained nights of no limits and the demon which has been latent is now unleashed. I am rough with poor Lilla. She turns away from me afterwards and her tears don't stop.

She is crying, "Why? Why do you hate me? It's not

my fault I look like her."

My little girl. What did I do?

I try to hold her. She pushes me away but I pull her tight to me and let her cry into my chest.

"Please don't leave me, I am so sorry. I lost myself in your beauty. I didn't mean to hurt you, really I didn't," I tell her.

"You hurt me," she says. "You were really rough tonight, István. I don't like it. All this biting and holding me down so I can't move. And you sucked my blood like a vampire from my shoulder. Why did you hurt me when I asked you to stop?"

"I am so sorry, my darling girl. I just love you too much. I could never hate you, please don't cry."

I am an animal and I am careless and cruel, but I do not mean to be most of the time.

But at other times I know I am cruel.

I am so careful after this as I know any more of this could send her back to her mother. I just handle her like a delicate doll. She comes home from school each day and takes care of Natalija until I get back from work. But she can't cook. She hasn't a clue. We have to eat out or if I have the energy, I cook. She leaves towels all over the bathroom floor. She leaves her school papers and magazines scattered in the living room.

I just clear them up. She is a child; I just need to gently turn her into an adult.

She eats potato chips and drops crumbs everywhere. She will give Natalija bad habits. I have made sure my daughter eats well and never has junk food. Lilla eats croissants in bed. This drives me mad. I tell her *the bed is no place for breakfast. Okay, have your croissants although I do not like them but for God's sake, Lilla we eat breakfast in the kitchen at the table. Set an example for Natalija,*

And please don't eat junk in the house. Natalija has

been brought up on good food and I have never once had a bag of potato chips or sweets in the cupboard. We can make cakes with good quality chocolate, but bad food is banned here. On no account mention junk food outlets because Natalija has been educated by me that these are places for unhealthy, ugly, fat people. If she wants to be beautiful, she is not to eat there. And you need to stay beautiful so you are to stay away from there too. I will make sure we eat healthy food. Nothing but fresh ingredients or the finest restaurants.

"Okay," Lilla says but I can see she is not happy. I don't mention the papers lying around or the wet towels. I am not going to lecture her anymore. But I don't want her bringing junk food into this apartment.

It is March and I am sad as I know what I need to do. I have to go to Pécs and visit Kiára's grave. March and April are the absolute worst months for me. Kiára's birthday was on the 1st April and she attempted suicide in March that terrible time I was in America for a conference and then one year later, died in April soon after her birthday. It was once my favourite time of year as the weather would start to lift into lightness and warmth but now I hate it for all the memories I have. I usually travel here in March and April as my love died when she attempted suicide and they restarted her heart twice, then for the final time the following April so both months are full of sadness. It is as though she died twice so I have double the pain.

And forever the guilt which is that I should have done more; I should not have left the country for work even for a week. If I had never gone to that stupid conference, she would not have attempted suicide. I called her every day and I had friends and an au pair go there 12 hours a day just to be sure she was safe while I was away. But she wasn't safe and I take all the blame. I have never forgiven myself. If I had stayed in Hungary she would still be alive.

I am sad to be living in Budapest which is the other end of the country to her grave but I could not deal with the memories in that small town. Every street, every restaurant reminded me of her until I felt I was imploding with grief which never ceased. I had to leave; I couldn't bear to stay with memories in the apartment and memories outside and nightmares all the time. Today we go together to visit her; me, Lilla and Natalija. It is the first time Lilla has asked me, as I drive us to the south what happened to my wife. I tell her she died of a cardiac arrest. It was a year after she had attempted suicide by jumping into the Duna River and her heart had been permanently damaged after the fall and just failed again with no warning. I woke up to find her body warm next to me but no pulse and no breath. As I say it I feel the tears falling down my face. It is the first time I have told anyone apart from a shrink exactly what happened as usually people do not ask me what happened when I say my wife died. Lilla reaches out and squeezes my hand. "That is so sad," she says. "So sad." She gently wipes a tear from my face.

She is so full of empathy despite her young age.

We arrange flowers in the cemetery and I can see Natalija is confused. "But mama is back," she says pointing at Lilla. She is only three years old now. I don't want to destroy her hope; that her mother came back for her so I decide I will have to explain it all when she is old enough to understand. Lilla arranges some flowers on the grave and sheds a few tears, "Poor Kiára. She was too young to die." She touches the marble stone with her gentle hands.

We sit a long time as it is a warm day, none of us speaking, not even Natalija who feels the sadness even though she cannot comprehend why. She touches the gravestone and looks at Lilla as if she is going to disappear. Maybe I shouldn't have brought her here. It is just confusing the poor little girl.

We drive back to Budapest in silence.

ICE PRINCESS

It is June and I am desperate to marry my Lilla. I am frenzied as I have only known her 5 months. I see her 18th birthday as a good age; she was 18 on 3rd June and I have showered her in expensive gifts and told her I love her more than anything but I have not told her that I am afraid I will lose her forever unless I tie her down now. I have come to realise that actually I don't love her yet; it is absolute raging obsession. Obsession because I have found my dead love's likeness in someone else. She has so many new clothes and shoes and designer underwear, I know I am buying her affection. She does seem to care for me and she tells me, "You are so handsome, István. So handsome and so kind."

We haven't had any arguments but there is something about Lilla that I cannot describe; there is an emptiness. Even when she shows happiness or affection there is a coolness about her as if she is not really connected with the world. Despite her devastating beauty which every man notices when we are out, there is something missing which I just feel but I cannot explain. I only sense its absence; I do not know what it is or maybe I am just paranoid. She seems to connect with sadness as when I have been crying over Kiára or Natalija is upset, she is like an animal that senses someone needs comforting. But other than this, there is something not quite real about her as if she isn't of this world.

Which leads me to believe that she must be the love of my life reincarnated. I am so convinced of it now. She came back for me.

Everyone would tell me what I am doing is madness. My shrink has told me *I will not find Kiára in this girl. It is not good for me and not good for her. I need to let her go.*

I tell him *no way will I ever let her go. I will cling on to her forever if I have to. I will do everything it takes to keep her.*

Now I have found my reincarnated dead love I am holding on to her. I will lock her up in our amber palace, my beautiful ice princess. She came back to me, my darling. She rose from the dead to be with me. She is not mortal.

The shrink says *I am starting to lose my grip on reality. I need to stop and reassess what I am doing at least, give it more time and slow it down* but I do not listen. He tells me *I am starting to go into mania.*

I want and I want and I want and it never ceases. My thoughts are racing further and further into the future and will not stop. This doctor doesn't understand I have to have her as mine now. I need to marry her now, not next year, or in 2 years. I have to have her.

One of my biggest worries is I am afraid Lilla will get bored and start to look at younger men once she starts her university course after the summer. She will study Literature and French and English and I am relieved she is not doing a demanding medical course; an arts course gives her a lot of free time. I want her to take care of Natalija. She had no doubt about staying in Budapest, she never even talked about applying to other universities but I have a desperation I never had with Kiára. When I met Kiára, I was cautious, despite my feelings as I knew she could slash my heart to pieces and it took me a long time to commit. Now I have found her image in this lovely young girl, I need to know I won't lose her; it would kill me.

I wish I could find some way to stop Lilla going to university as I worry that it could be the end for us. She will enter a different world. At school, she doesn't really fit in; she is bored, beautiful and doesn't have many friends but I know at university it is likely she will be surrounded by a range of attractive young men and women and will start to question our relationship. It is crucial I do something, anything to imprison her.

I have come to see her as a mythical creature and I don't want her mixing with mortal beings. I do not tell anyone this, least of all my shrink.

Lilla agrees when I ask her to marry me in a romantic restaurant in Budapest but in a way that doesn't show delight, just thoughtfulness. "Of course, I would like that," she says.

Just for that evening I have left Natalija with the au pair. I want to show Lilla I am serious and I need us to be alone. I just tell Natalija I have a surprise for her when she says hurt, "But you always take me."

"You will see, Natalija," I tell her and I am terrified Lilla will say no as I say it. And I know it is not a going to be a surprise for Natalija because as far as she can see, her mother is with us all the time, she would not understand marriage. I will just tell her we are having a party on our wedding day and dress her up like a princess.

Lilla opens the box holding the engagement ring and says it is beautiful but she doesn't say she loves me. She just says *she is very happy* as she tries on her ring and holds the diamond up to the candlelight admiring the rainbow, the trick of the light trapped in the cold stone. I measured her finger with dental floss as she was sleeping one night so I could get exactly the right size and surprise her like this. The magical moment falls completely flat; no stars or angel dust floating in the air. No passion from Lilla. I also feel nothing. It was expensive, this large rock but she wouldn't know a cheap gift store ring from the most expensive diamond in the world. Maybe I should have spent less. Maybe I should have used Kiára's rings, the ones I was saving for Natalija when she is older but somehow to use my dead love's engagement ring seemed badly wrong. It would make our relationship fated from the start. I do not see that it is already fated as I am marrying her for all the wrong reasons. I do not want to see, more like.

I am convinced that she is the answer to my world despite the empty feeling I have right now.

I remind myself that Lilla has never known love. I am her first and I want to be her last but I expected more excitement in her answer and this makes me angry. But we drink champagne and she seems dizzy and happy as I carry her into the apartment and she rests her head on my chest.

She says, "I am yours now, István. I am yours."

Yes, you are. You are mine until the day you die. Or I die. Or we both die in the flames of my raging passion and jealousy, molten together as one flesh. Like lovers who dive into a volcano together.

I hope you know what you are doing, my darling girl.

I dress her in beautiful brilliant white, glittering jewels in her hair and I still have the feeling Natalija is more excited than Lilla on the wedding day. I had it booked ready for only two weeks after I asked her to marry me as I was so sure she would not refuse. Or maybe I wasn't certain, I just couldn't bear to think of her saying no. Natalija is happy at this party. She is devoted to Lilla. Lilla is merely cool and content. She is a real ice princess. Beautiful, delicate but her heart doesn't seem to be warm. I have visions that it is not even beating, that I have imagined she is real and she is just a figment of my distressed imagination. I start to feel I am losing my mind. It is the first real unravelling I have experienced. Sure, I fell apart after Kiára's death and I have existed in a mist until I met

Lilla but this is a splintering feeling. As though I am cracking like a mirror and shards of my personality are starting to fall to the ground.

I know I am being paranoid. I have been cutting back on my medication as it has been dulling my mind, sometimes interfering with my thinking and I need to be sharp for dental and facial surgery as I work early in the mornings. As I have been taking on more complex facial surgery cases it is essential for my mind to be scalpel sharp. I do not see this is the worst thing I can do, cutting back on my medication. I reason that I have been better now I have found this girl so maybe I don't need all these meds which I still hide from Lilla. I hide them from Natalija for her own safety as she is very inquisitive at her age so hiding them from Lilla seems normal.

Afterwards I ask Lilla *is she happy, does she love me?* She has just sworn to stay with me forever and she seems indifferent as we walk out into the hot July sun. Budapest has the feeling of a dragon's mouth today and the heat is unpleasant and oppressive and there are a lot of storms this month. She is an ice princess in the burning sun but her heart seems to be frozen. I am too hot in my black suit. She is not even warm, her hands are cool to the touch and the diamond sparkles cold on her hand. I have a panic attack as I start to think I am imagining the whole experience and Lilla will vanish like a snow queen in one of the fairy tales she reads to Natalija every night. I am gasping for air and Lilla gets me into a taxi and says, "You are just too hot, István. It is over 30c and you are wearing a black wool suit."

I swallow two klonopin with a bottle of water and I hear Natalija's voice distant and stretchy asking, "István, what's wrong?"

Lilla hugs the little girl and says *nothing is wrong, he is dressed in black and he is too hot.*

"We are ice queens in white, you and me Natalija," she tells her.

Natalija is satisfied by this and plays with her doll.

"I love you, you know I do," Lilla says softly into my ear as we head home out of this burning Hellhole of the city centre. She has not asked for anything; no expensive wedding, no gifts or exotic holidays but I am still angry. I look at the beautiful sapphire necklace round her throat which was once my first gift to Kiára and right now I can only see Kiára but something is not right with all this. *I am not right with all this.*

I suddenly feel rage smouldering within me and I want to hurt her as she sits there calm and white, my new bride. My rediscovered Kiára. I want to hurt her so badly. I want to gently take off her white dress and necklace and fuck her until she begs me to stop. I want to violate her in every way possible. Then I see her smile at me in the taxi and she slips her cold hand into mine and I feel horrible guilt for the violent thoughts which I didn't think I would feel again. I hurt Kiára more than I should at times, we hurt each other and now I am having those awful thoughts returning. I do not like this side of me. I am a sadist and I hurt everyone who gets close to my heart.

She reads Natalija a bedtime story, my perfect white princess, my snow queen still in her lovely dress. I wouldn't let her take it off and Natalija begged her to keep it on so I let them both leave on their dresses whereas I cannot wait to get out of this hot black Armani suit and put the air conditioning on full blast. As Lilla reads the story, Natalija gazes up at her as if she is the most beautiful woman in the world. She is no longer a girl, my Lilla. She is a woman and now I can treat her like one. The thoughts are screaming in my head. The two conflicting voices are shouting *protect this lovely girl* and the other is to *hurt her like Hell, show her who is boss.*

Later, I gently unhook Lilla's dress and necklace under the flickering light of black candles in the bedroom. "Black is a bit dark for a wedding night," says Lilla suddenly. She looks at the candles burning like a sacrificial altar.

"I am dark, Lilla, you should know that by now," I say kissing her golden neck and shoulders but I am feeling full of venom tonight. She can't see my expression and I know it is dark and angry. The demon is waiting to be unleashed. "I am very dark, baby."

"What do you mean by dark? I know you like black but it was a bit stupid to wear a black suit on such a hot day," says Lilla and there is fear in her voice for the first time.

Stupid, baby? Did you call me stupid? I will show you what I mean by dark. You are not real anyway, I can do what I want tonight as tomorrow you might have vanished back into my dark imagination. Did I create you Lilla? Did I dream you up just to ease my savagely broken heart?

The night has a feeling of unreality.

I hold her down and grab her wrists and tie them gently to the bedframe and I see for the first time there is fear in her eyes but she says nothing, not a word of protest. So I do everything I want to do as long as I want to do it. I feel my body turning to liquid, my mind is almost losing consciousness; I feel the power of centuries flowing through my veins and I have everything I need. My fragments are all merging together to make one wonderful whole and I lose myself, forgetting everything but the moment and her flesh. I can't hear Lilla, I just taste and feel and smell her skin and perfume and her body is mine. It is only when I am sliding back into reality that I hear her crying, first as though it is coming from a long distance away and then suddenly it is close and I am back in my body and back in the moment, and her tears are on my skin.

"Baby, what happened, what did I do?" I don't even know myself what I did. I was so wrapped up in her sweet tender flesh, feeling as though time had stopped.

"You hurt me. You forced me. And I thought you loved me," she keeps saying over and over. She is too broken into fragments, my delicate ice girl. She has been crying for an hour and I have been trying to calm her.

She turns towards me and asks, "Why did you marry me to do things like that? I didn't even know you could do such stuff to someone you loved. You were so gentle when I met you. You were my first. If this is love then I don't want it. I don't want it." Her make-up has run down her face and she is in pain.

I am hateful. I am an animal. I hate myself.

I have been given another chance at happiness and this is what I do.

"I want my mother," she says. "I want my mother."

Her mother refused to attend the wedding and told Lilla on the phone if she has a child with me then her life is as good as over. I am the Devil incarnate. Her mother hates me as much as though a crackhead married her daughter. I have tried to call her and tell her *Lilla is happy, I am taking care of her and I have plenty of money. She doesn't need to worry.*

She tells me *I will ruin Lilla's life and she is so young and should be dating men her own age.*

She even says, "Don't think I am going to see the devil child you give her. I do not want a grandchild from you. You should be ashamed of what you have done. Your daughter could be a sister to Lilla, they are that close in age."

What exactly is it I have done?

What has she ever done for Lilla?

I am angry with this uneducated woman who lives in some hole in a gloomy area of town telling me this. I have given Lilla everything. She has a beautiful apartment to live in, money and happiness. If it weren't for Lilla I would love to tell this Ágnes witch to fuck off. But I don't want Lilla upset,

Ágnes is still her mother after all.

But on our wedding night after I let all my passion, love, anger and hate fuse into one and push our love to its limits I know exactly what I have done. I am a demon and my beautiful Lilla is crying so hard I think my heart will break

And now Lilla is not happy on what should be the happiest day of her life.

This is something else I have stolen from her. I have stolen her purity and now stolen her right to have a wonderful wedding night. I will keep taking everything from her until there is nothing left.

She could have asked me for an expensive holiday or expensive gifts but she asked for nothing more than love and I have not given her that. Or more like I have, but in my own twisted way.

"Lilla, my darling Lilla. I hurt you because I love you too much. I am so sorry. I have no excuse," I tell her. "I am so sad I hurt you. I really didn't mean to, I got lost in your beautiful body. Please forgive me, baby."

I hold her tight and she lets me because she is too destroyed to do anything else. I lick the tears from her face and keep holding her, stroking her hair. I have another insane idea that maybe having a child with Lilla might be a good idea. Right now I want my new bride to give me a son, after all she promised to give me children in our wedding vows so why not now? All my family are dead and I need a son to carry on my bloodline. I am frenzied as if I need everything this minute. But as I ask her that night, I know that Lilla will not agree. She takes her pill religiously now. She is shocked especially given my aggression that night and says *she adores Natalija, she is too young for a child and why am I even asking?*

"Because it's our wedding night, Lilla. You said you would give me children in your wedding vows earlier," I tell her. "Wouldn't it be a good time?"

"Please not yet. I love you, István but I hadn't even thought about it and now you really hurt me and it isn't the first time you hurt me," she says.

"I am so sorry I hurt you. Lilla, I love you, please forgive me," I say and I just hold her. My poor girl and my twisted sadistic love.

I know that I am wanting one more way to trap her in the razor wire of my heart and keep her there forever. I am holding my damaged young wife and wanting her to have my child, one as beautiful as Natalija, as if that will fix everything. She is eighteen and I am a controlling monster.

I keep ruining our sweetness with my sexual aggression. I have to start seeing the shrink more often and working through this as the pattern repeats itself again and again with a murderous intensity.

Lilla falls asleep in my arms, softening and moving closer. Honey skin and long limbs wrapping around me. "Forgive me, I love you," I say into her beautiful black eyelashes. "You are my life, my whole life. I have been waiting for you for so long."

This last bit is not entirely true. I waited a lifetime for my Queen, Kiára and the second I saw her when I was 40 years old, I knew I wanted her forever. But as Lilla is Kiára's image, I could say I have been waiting my whole life for her.

I even find in her medical records she is blood group O negative. My heart races; *the same as me, the same as Kiára.* It is a rare blood group in Hungary. I knew it. She has to be Kiára brought back to life. No wonder I want to suck her sweet blood.

I oversleep due to worrying late into the night and it is Saturday and I wake up to an empty bed and no Lilla. I leap out in wild panic as I am convinced Lilla has left already. Or I was right and she was just a figment of my frenzied mind working overtime. She has been married one day and she has gone. I can hardly breathe. I have to get her back. I am hyperventilating as I run into the kitchen where I can hear voices.

My damaged ice princess is in the kitchen with Natalija, making her breakfast. She can at least make toast and Nutella if nothing else although she even burns the toast sometimes. She turns to see me in the doorway and looks away hurt, without smiling at me. She looks so beautiful and her hair is still held up with diamond pins as she didn't have a chance to unravel it all last night, although it looks a bit dishevelled, the only sign she has been mauled by an absolute animal overnight. My guilt and shame bite into me.

"My darling," I say. "My darling Lilla."

"István," shouts Natalija. "Can we still have the party today?"

Yes of course, I tell her. I kiss her and say *this whole weekend is officially a party for all of us.*

I go over to Lilla and take her hand.

"Why does she call you by your name?" asks Lilla. It is the first time she has questioned me about this.

I tell her *Kiára wanted Natalija to call us by our names and besides I did not want to be called 'Apa'. I want her to call me by my name; that is who I am. If Natalija wants to call Lilla 'mama', fine but I am not going to be called 'Apa'. Anyone could be called 'Apa' and I am not anyone.*

Lilla looks away. She is upset after yesterday, like

a wounded animal. She pulls her hand from mine gently and then starts to get my breakfast out of the fridge for me. I stop her and hold her tight and whisper that *I love her more than anything.*

"Please forgive me, Lilla, please. You are my world," I tell her as I brush away a loose wave of her dark hair from her face. I see a cruel bite on her neck where I sucked on her sweet blood and I want to turn back the clock and do everything all again, but her way.

I take her face in my hands and look into her lovely brown eyes and see the hurt I caused but she holds me and says *she loves me, she will forgive me but she thinks I need help.* This last bit is serious. *She is worried about me, she is in too deep to get out but I need help.*

"You hurt mama," says Natalija suddenly without looking up from her toast. It isn't angry or accusing just a simple fact.

"Did you tell her that?" I say to Lilla.

She doesn't answer, just points to the bite on her neck and passes me my freshly squeezed vegetable juice. Why did Lilla tell her it was me? I wish she had made something up.

I don't want to say anything and make it worse. I don't want Natalija to know any more than she already does. She is too perceptive for her age, too smart. I don't want my daughter to know I am a sadistic lover but as she gets older she will find out more and more. I just hope she never turns against me as I have treated her like a princess since she lost her mother. Natalija was all I had until now.

I go to shave and I look in the mirror at the monster I have become. My hair hangs in jet black corkscrew curls and my eyes are so dark I cannot see the pupil even in this light. Creamy skin and perfect teeth; I look ten years younger and I know people see me as very handsome. Kiára said I was the most beautiful man on earth. I was arrogant when I was younger as women would fall for me all the time but I cast them all aside very quickly. They were nothing to me. I hurt them and I didn't care if they were in love with me. I think of all those women I just cast aside after a week, two weeks, maybe three if they were exceptional and all of them cried and asked me, "Why? Why?"

I didn't know. I would always say, "I am sorry, sweetheart. I don't love you and I don't think I ever will."

I would leave them broken-hearted. I didn't mean to cause such suffering but I couldn't love. I only loved sex until I met Kiára.

And then I only ever loved Kiára. *My life, my love, my everything.*

Now this new lovely reincarnation of my dead love who told me one evening 'You are so beautiful' as if I were a painting and not a real flesh and blood being has been tricked by my attractive outer shell. She did not see the demon within and the dark damaged heart.

But I look in the mirror straight through the handsome outer shell and see the demon inside. I am cruel and I hurt everyone who tries to love me. Even my long lost beautiful Queen. I lean over to wash my face.

The end of July heat is pushing 40c and the nights are full of electric storms. I am snappy, frenzied and waking early in the morning. I am trying to be gentle as I love Lilla as she is still half-asleep and she murmurs, "Oh, István, I am so tired. Please let me sleep more." But she lets me do what I want. I would do it anyway as in my manic states I am always wanting more and more sex. I am telling Lilla I am King István and I am full of ideas past and present.

She is puzzled; she studied history at school and knows Hungarian history but is confused or thinks I am making up stories for fun. I am serious. I have ideas of setting up a clinic to treat depression with blood transfusions and I am convinced I can do this. I even start to make little models of my clinic out of Lego bricks. I have bought the Lego for me and Lilla is puzzled, asking me why and she thought the Lego was for Natalija as I return home from the toy shop with boxes and boxes of the stuff. I don't speak as I am lost in concentration. Natalija wants to help but I tell her this is very serious business as I click and snap the bricks together at the kitchen table. She sits there watching me, her dark eyes serious but knowing that I mean what I say. At night I carefully place the Lego clinic on the top shelf of our wardrobe in case Natalija gets hold of it. I cannot have my ideas touched by anyone else. I will go mad with rage. This is my idea.

At night I am planning my battles from the year 1000 in my sleep as the nightmares are returning and I am shouting and Lilla has to wake me and tell me I am okay, it is a bad dream. Kiára always had to comfort me through my nightmares as I didn't take any medication until after her suicide attempt so I had nightmares and vivid dreams about being King István every single night. This time, I don't put it down to my meds or cutting back on them. I feel my mind is razor sharp as I concentrate without the usual mist which clouds my thoughts. I am racing and it feels good, too good. I could be scraped off the ceiling as I picture myself like a helium balloon but I will not come down. In the spare moments in the evening, I am planning for this clinic where we can cure the endemic disease of depression; alone I can save Hungary past and present and future. I am determined I can cure our nation of its gloom and the thought makes me feel powerful. I am arrogant and although I know people do not like me in work generally, I am more unpopular right now because they seem to be speaking very slowly and I get impatient in meetings and start finishing everyone's sentences for them. Sometimes I say, "For God's sake, hurry up and tell us already."

I am rude, difficult and speedy. I am making inappropriate comments about sex to the young dental assistants. I don't want them, I am not trying to pick them up; I just think I am making everyday conversation and the poor girls are so embarrassed they drop boxes in the treatment room and pass me the wrong equipment in their nervousness. They are too afraid to say much to me and they certainly would not report me due to my senior position. Right now I have no concept of bipolar. I believe I am cured as I am feeling so good, so fucking good. I have a lovely young wife *who* is only 18 years old and I can have her every night. How many men my age could possess someone so perfect? I bring in Lilla one day just to show her off.

One dental assistant says *Lilla looks young enough to be my daughter*. She says it to embarrass me as Lilla is younger than all the staff there. I do not care. I say *Lilla is very mature for her age*.

She is my prize, my jewels, my reincarnated Queen. "This is my Lilla," I tell them as I wrap my arm around her shoulders. "My beautiful wife."

And I am demanding more and more from Lilla and I have a memory from this time which is her saying, "Please. Not again. My darling, I love you but I need to sleep. Morning and night you are wanting it and I am exhausted and when you can't sleep, in the middle of the night too. You were never like this before. Where are you getting your energy from?"

Fragments

From the centuries of blood flowing through me as I do not need to sleep. I have so much power within me it is never going to stop.

Then I remember nothing as reality slowly slides away. I just feel colours racing by; thoughts are balloons in different colours floating high and I am up there. I am speeding. I am up there with the balloons trying to catch the words and colours and I see everyone below moving so slowly, talking so slowly and I have a memory of shouting, "I am King again!" Somehow there is a lot of cereal on the kitchen floor and someone is crying and this is the last thing I remember.

I want the blue balloon. I want it and I want it now. It drifts above me, just out of my grasp.

Then blackness.
I am stopped.

HOSPITAL

I wake up in hospital. Kiára is sitting by my bed. She is crying. It is 14th August Kiára tells me. I reach for her hand and pain shoots through my wrist. I raise my arm but it is so heavy and such an effort. It is bandaged as is the other. I am so drugged up I cannot remember what happened. I am frightened as I have no memory and no memory of what time of year it is but outside the trees have leaves and the sun is bright and high so it must be August.

I have lost a lot of time somewhere and I want to get it back. Kiára tells me I was drawing battle plans on the wall in thick black magic marker a week ago in the living room. I was very ill. She had to call an ambulance as I was shouting that I was no longer the King. She was so afraid as the paramedics took me away and I fell out of the bed the other day and hurt my wrists. This doesn't sound right. There is something missing. I lost a chunk of time. I just remember speeding, talking very fast and feeling like I owned the world and I do not know how I am in the hospital. It was all going great.

I was sure it was all going great. I have a memory of it all being great. I was the King. How did I end up lying in bed with marshmallow stuffed into my brain. It is spongey and all the thoughts are sticking together in this mallow gloop.

There is a blue balloon floating high above my bed. Kiára sees me looking at it and says, "Natalija brought it for you. She thought you would like a balloon if you were ill. She filled the living room with balloons for you to come back to. I hope you don't mind."

"I like balloons, you know I do, Kiára," I say brightly. I remember why I like balloons.

This lovely Lilla as she is insists she is now called,

says *that night I was admitted to hospital was horrible, really horrible. I was so frenzied and out of control and I had a wild look in my eyes and she was terrified, not for her safety but for me. I was so strong and out of control. She kept trying to hold me and calm me down but I was breaking loose and running around the apartment.*

"I found your medicine stashed in the top of the wardrobe, István. You had so many pills you hadn't taken for 2 months. The hospital told me you are sick with bipolar one," she says. "I didn't know you were so sick. I told them in work you had kidney problems and you were admitted. How could I tell them you were taken to a psychiatric ward? How could I tell them my husband was crazy?"

That hurts; crazy. She thinks I am crazy. Not creative, not even sick, just crazy.

"Natalija, where is Natalija?" I ask.

"She is with the au pair," says Kiára. She looks so young.

"Kiára, I am so sorry," I say fuzzy from the meds.

"I am Lilla, your new wife," Kiára tells me. "Don't you remember me? Do I really only exist to you as your dead love?" She cries some more.

"That's the only reason you married me, because I am like her. How can I live up to her? How can I live up to someone dead? She will always be better than me in your eyes. Always."

I have a vague memory of this beautiful girl, delicate as crystal in a white dress but I see only Kiára. I wonder how much I have dreamed up. Who is this crystal ice princess my love is telling me about?

"Please don't leave me, baby," I tell her. "You are my world. My love, my life."

I catch her tears in my hands, those diamond tears of hers.

She holds my hand gently and tells me she will

help me get well no matter what it takes.

"I have to go now but I will be back tomorrow. The hospital needs you here for a week at least to stabilise you. I wish you had told me about your medicine, I wish you had told me how sick you were. I had to look it up on the internet. I didn't even know why you were going so strange," says this lovely Lilla. My ice princess. *I remember now; she is my ice princess and she lives in a palace made of amber.*

But somehow I have made her so sad.

"Don't go, please don't leave me," I say. "You can't leave me alone like this."

I try to push the sheets aside and say, "Can you just come in here a minute, baby. I want you next to me. Let me show you I love you. I will really love you if you just get into this bed and I can hold you and show you what I am feeling."

"István, I can't. You are in hospital," she says. She sounds shocked as if I suggested something really crazy. "You can't have sex in a hospital bed. Why are you like this? Is everything sex to you?"

I am hurt. I am in bed, why can't she join me?

She can't look at me. She just kisses my lips and strokes a curl of hair away from my eyes as she leaves telling me *she and Natalija are repainting the desecrated living room wall I covered in black magic marker. She is too ashamed to ask a decorator to do it.*

I am drifting away.

"Please come back, please don't leave me," I drawl. My tongue is thick from the medication. But I slide into unconsciousness.

Everything goes black again. They have drugged me. They have stolen away my soul.

They have taken away my power. I am weak.

They are releasing me after 2 weeks on condition I see my doctor weekly and Lilla is to make sure I take my meds. I am supposed to stay longer but I tell them

Fragments

I have my wife to care for me.

I have remembered that I have a new wife, my reincarnated love called Lilla.

Some of the staff look doubtful when Lilla arrives to take me home as she is young. They thought she was my daughter bringing her younger sister to visit each day. No one really seemed to register she was my wife.

Poor Natalija seeing me like this. I have not remembered much here either but I do remember Natalija on the bed with her toy dinosaurs asking w*hat was wrong?*

I was just a bit sick, we tell her. *Not to worry, I will be fine.* As if I just had a touch of flu.

But the balloon helps, I say cheerfully.

Good, says Natalija. *You get me balloons when I am sick.*

Lilla just looks at the balloon sadly.

They have whacked me up to maximum dose of these meds. I am dull and fuzzy. I had a psychotic episode, a combination of summer heat and sun and cutting down drastically on my tablets. In the taxi Lilla tells me what really happened that night. I drew battle plans on the wall in magic marker, I was ranting and shouting and dumping boxes of cereal and pasta all over the kitchen floor in big heaps. I woke Natalija who started crying. As Lilla went to see to Natalija I cut my wrists in the bathroom and wet my pajamas like a child. She was nearly as hysterical as me as she tried to patch up my wrists and change my clothes.

"I cut my wrists," I say in horror. "My God, I might never work again! I could have damaged my tendons, I am ruined. My career is over." I am in a blind panic trying to pull apart the bandages on my wrists. I cannot understand this as I cannot remember. I don't remember being suicidal.

Lilla holds my hands still and strokes my face. She couldn't tell me until now as she didn't want to scare me.

"No, it is okay. The paramedics and the hospital told me it was superficial. We will change the dressings and I will show you, but István you can't work for a month at least, not because of your wrists but because you are sick," she says.

Maybe the fact I wasn't suicidal when I cut my wrists stopped me making a serious attempt which could have proved the end of my medical career. I am afraid; the thought makes me ill. I will never ever stop medication again.

And why was I wearing pajamas? This is one big thing I cannot work out. I have pajamas and I only wear them when I am sick or when Lilla stayed the first weekend with me and I wanted her to think I was not going to seduce her.

"Lilla, why was I wearing pajamas?" I ask after a few minutes' silence.

She takes her time to answer, "Because you were running around the apartment naked and threatened to go into the street. I put them on you. How could I let your daughter or the neighbours see you so crazy?" She wipes her eyes with a tissue. "I would have been so ashamed."

What about me? Respected dentist and surgeon running around naked in the street in the middle of an August night. I would never be able to speak to the neighbours again.

Lilla looks out of the taxi window. I have betrayed her. I have hurt her.

Everyone has been asking am I okay in the dental surgery and Lilla has had to lie and tell them I had kidney trouble. But I know they saw me acting manic before I went to hospital. I hope they don't know. I hope they don't guess.

Fragments

I am ashamed. I am still holding the blue balloon Natalija brought for me. It floats on the taxi ceiling and reminds me of how I was soaring before they drugged me and made me fuzzy and heavy.

It is national holiday, ironically Szent István day on 20th August but I am not feeling like Szent István right now and we are not going anywhere. It is probably just as well that we have this break although I was supposed to attend a conference in Zurich. I am in danger of not attending enough conferences which will put my dental licence at risk. Kiára or Lilla as she insists she is called, gently changes my wrist bandages and shows me the small scars.

"See, they are not deep. You will be okay soon," she says.

I reach for her hair and stroke her face. She tells me *she would not have married me so soon if she knew about all this. It is too much for her. She loves me but she is young and this has shaken her up*. I know that she married me too soon after meeting me, due to her being so child-like and me being wildly impulsive.

"Don't think I don't love you, István but you swept me away when I met you. You were so handsome, so sure of yourself. I didn't know all this was hiding under the surface. I never knew you could fall apart like this," she is crying again. *My darling girl*.

"Please never leave me; I am so sorry I put you through so much. I don't know what I would have done about Natalija if I was in hospital," I tell her.

"And you wanted me to have another child as well. How can you even think of that when we are in this state? I'm 18, István. I am going to university and I have to take care of Natalija and now you. What were you thinking of?" She says this more sadly than accusatory.

I am confused. "We do have a child, our little girl."

Kiára or Lilla says nothing, just brushes the curls from my face and says *she made a commitment, she will take care of me and Natalija but I am never to cut out medicine again. She will make sure I take my tablets.*

She will make sure I stay well.

She brought Natalija to see me every day in hospital or maybe it is just one day and I keep reliving it and Natalija wants to know what happened.

I just tell her *I am sick, the doctors needed to take care of me for a short time and then everything will be okay.* She looks sad and confused, my little girl. She had wanted to go to Lake Balaton and I was supposed to go to a conference in Zurich. I am so angry with myself. If I do not attend enough conferences I will risk having my dental licence taken away and I am going to have to work even harder to make up this lost time. I was going to go to the 2 week conference and then join Lilla and Natalija in Lake Balaton for a few days. I know this was the plan.

I force myself to go back to work earlier than my doctors recommend. They tell me I will risk getting ill again but I cannot take time off. No one knows or has guessed about my illness. They think I am strange, rude and difficult. I would rather they thought that. On 4th September I return to work and I do not remember what Lilla says she told the surgery was wrong with me when they ask am I better.

I just say *I am very angry with myself for getting sick and missing the conference in Switzerland* and do not say anything else. I am fuzzy and my balance is totally off. I am not supposed to drive on all these increased meds but after a tram journey where I overbalance and stand on everyone's feet and have to keep apologising I am never taking public transport again, I should have just taken a taxi. I had to go downtown for a meeting but usually I can walk to the surgery which is 10 minutes from my house. I do not need the car for work so once the meds are stabilising me, I will be able to drive if we need to go anywhere. Fuck it. I just need an entire pot of coffee to function before work as I am so sleepy in the morning.

CONTROL

It is September and before the light and sun start to die, I manage to drive us to Tihany on Lake Balaton as the weather is still warm and has lost its oppressive summer heat. I feel so bad for Natalija missing out on the holiday, I promised I would take us there for the weekend. But I should not be driving on all these meds; if we are stopped by the cops I am screwed. I will have to bribe them in order to keep my licence. I keep thinking if I try to act normal this illness will go away. I am still in denial after all these years.

Lilla begins her university course and I am trying to work medicated up to the maximum dose and fuzzy which makes me angry and I have to drink caffeine to be alert enough for work and all I can think of is the young men she will meet and I am simmering with vitriolic jealousy already. She returns after her first few days and starts to talk about being invited to a party that weekend.

"No way," I say as we eat our sushi. Goddamn girl can't cook, I am not used to all this take-out food even when it is healthy. I want to get home from work and have my dinner waiting.

"No way, Lilla. You are not going to any drunken student party. The men will be all over you. You are **MY** wife," I say and point at her with the chopsticks. "You are mine. *Mine.*"

"But I said I would go," Lilla says hurt. She is not angry. She doesn't have the fire of Kiára, due to her age and inexperience and I know she will not disobey my orders.

"You are not a student beyond your class hours, Lilla. You are my wife and Natalija thinks you are her mother. You are not to go anywhere at night without me," I tell her firmly.

Lilla looks down and she is upset but I know she will listen. She has no choice. I am boss.

"And Lilla, I am going to pay for a cookery course for you because I am sick of this. You can hardly make toast and Nutella for Natalija. I like eating out and the cleaner brings us home-made dishes but I just want to get home one day or two days a week and fucking well eat a nice dinner cooked by my wife. You are useless in the kitchen."

She sits with tears in her eyes.

"Don't worry, baby," I squeeze her hand. "You will like the cookery course. I did the same one and learned a lot; it's enjoyable. I will book you in for weekends." I feel bad for being angry with her. She cared for me when I was sick.

I take her to the most expensive restaurants in Budapest. She has not had anyone do this. Her mother could not afford to and she is full of wonder. I give her the finest wine to try and it makes her shed her coolness and laugh a lot more. I introduce her to foreign food she has never tasted. I buy her gifts; perfume, underwear, beautiful dresses and shoes from designer stores on Andrássy Út.

Each evening she talks excitedly about the university and the course and the people she has met. But I have no interest. She is just a girl. I am bored with her talk and she has no interest in my work although she patiently listens when I tell her about my day. However, she does not understand anything about the world of work or dentistry so it is really lost on her. I leave her for 2 weeks and go to America for an important conference and I am happy to leave her. I need a break from her incessant university chatter and I need to do this course. I call her every evening to speak to her and Natalija and they are both sweet but I feel like I talk as little to Lilla as I do to my daughter, who will only be 4 years old in December.

Without seeing Lilla and her loveliness, I am lost for words. I realise then that we have nothing really to say to each other. I am not consumed by jealousy as Lilla is in the apartment taking care of Natalija every single time I call. She is not out, even at the weekends when I call her twice a day and I am satisfied she is listening to what I tell her. She is obedient. She is not chasing after university boys.

When I get back from the airport, Lilla is not home and I am calling and calling her cell phone. It is a Friday night in October and 7pm and I know that she finished classes at 4pm today. I am angry and jet-lagged and hurt that she is not here to welcome me. I am trying to rationalise that she may just be having coffee somewhere or her lectures were overrunning but I can't. I am in a rage and I snap at Natalija who wants me to play with her. The little girl bursts into tears and I lift her up telling her *I am so sorry. I am not feeling too well.* I play with some dinosaurs just to try to get my mind off this raging fire of obsession which is eating away at me.

Natalija is drifting off to sleep and I get a call at 8pm. A girl called Krisztina is asking *am I the dentist, Lilla's husband? Lilla has passed out at a bar. She has drunk too much and she needs to get home. They are worried. She is very drunk.*

I am furious. I scoop Natalija out of her bed in her duvet and put her in the car and drive into the downtown. I call Krisztina from outside the bar and tell her *I am waiting outside, can they manage to bring Lilla out.*

A young man, no doubt one of those plying her with drink carries her out unassisted followed by another man and a girl. She dangles lifeless in his arms, her long hair hanging loose and her silver dress sparkling and I get out of the car and take her from him. I turn my vitriol on these young people. "How dare you let her get this way? She is a good girl. She is my wife and she is pure. She was a virgin when she met me unlike the rest of you who no doubt sleep around. You have no right. What did you do?"

The girl who phoned me, Krisztina says *she is so sorry but Lilla had some pálinka and she passed out. She just drank too much, nothing more. It is okay.* She hands me Lilla's beaded evening bag.

"Okay?" I shout. "You call this okay? She is my wife! She belongs with me, do you understand?"

The students look afraid and say, "Yes, Doktor Úr. We won't let her do it again."

"Damn right you won't," I snarl at them. "You will all stay away from my wife in future. She belongs at home with me." Maybe I shouldn't have disclosed that Lilla was a virgin when I met her. I don't usually disclose my personal life to people but I wanted to emphasise that Lilla is not like them, she will not be like them. She is pure. And I am determined she will not see these people again.

I stuff Lilla in the car roughly and have to fasten her seatbelt as she is flopping over.

I slap her face to try to wake her up but she is too drunk.

She is trying to say something. I am so angry I cannot speak. But I am worried she has drunk too much and I will have to make her throw up. She seems in a very bad way. I needn't worry. Halfway home she throws up all over herself in the front seat. It wakes her up momentarily.

"So sorry, I ..."

"Lilla, you goddamn drunken slut. What the fuck were you thinking of? And look at the mess in my fucking car!"

I accelerate harder up the road and Natalija wakes up with all the shouting and starts to cry in the backseat.

Lilla throws up again. *Fucking Hell. This will take forever to clean up.*

"I leave for two weeks, Lilla. Two weeks. I am tired from the flight and hoped you would be at home to welcome me. Instead you are drunk in a bar with God knows who. I am so angry." I slap the steering wheel as I tell her.

She is sliding down in her seat and I want to shake the sense out of her.

We reach the II district and I carry Natalija in first leaving Lilla slumped in her seat. I soothe Natalija's tears and put her to bed. I am so angry I feel like leaving Lilla in the car overnight but I am worried she might choke on her vomit or sober up and run away. As I lock the apartment to return to the car a neighbour tries to talk to me. I am abrupt and say *my wife is ill, she ate some bad oysters in a restaurant and I have to get her*. I am ashamed to admit she is just a drunken student.

I open the door and Lilla has sobered up a little to drawl *she is sorry, please forgive me, I didn't know what happened. I will clean up....*

"Shut up, Lilla," I say as I pick her up from the front seat and carry her upstairs. I am getting vomit on my suit and I am madder than Hell. I will have to wash the goddamn car myself.

In the apartment I drop her in the bath and spray water on her face and shower her in her clothes soaping up her hair. She is wearing a silver dress and sparkly shoes and this makes me madder as she probably didn't wear it in lectures. She obviously planned to go out and took the dress in her bag. I bought her that for me to see her in, not these testosterone fuelled boys. I am her husband and I have been away for two weeks and she is not there to welcome me on my return. *Selfish little bitch.* I would be there waiting for her if she had to travel away for only two days, let alone two weeks.

"István, I am sorry, I..." she cries. "I feel so ill, I will never drink again."

I rub her roughly with the towel and take off her wet clothes. I leave her lying in the recovery position on the bathroom floor in a towel and tell her *if she has to throw up, make the toilet for God's sake.*

It takes me an hour to clean her mess out of the car. As I am doing this I have resolved to drag Lilla out of university and get her to take the job vacancy as receptionist in our dental surgery. I am not having her mixing with these people, especially these young men. My jealousy is burning and burning so much it hurts my chest.

I am so disgusted with her. I never saw Kiára drunk. She only ever drank wine with me although I know when she was Lilla's age she was probably in the same state on a Friday night.

In the apartment she has managed to get up and clean her teeth. I tell her not to talk to me, get into bed and shut up. I can't even bear to sleep next to her but I am worried she is in danger of throwing up again as she might not have got it out of her system. I place her carefully on her side at the edge of the bed with a bucket below. If she throws up on my carpet I will fucking kill her. I curl up as far away as I can on the other side of the bed but in the night I move closer and I am holding her when I wake up in the morning.

She spends the next day in bed and throws up several times. I worry someone spiked her drink and I ask her more concerned *does she remember?*

She says *she remembers only drinking about 4 shots then it went black.*

I feel less angry but I know I am not letting her out of my sight again.

I also feel sorry for her feeling so bad. I bring her

soup and all I want to do that night is climb into bed and be gentle with her, show her my love. She can't get up until Sunday morning. She has been well and truly poisoned.

This weekend in October is the only emotional scene I have witnessed from Lilla; that Sunday as we are having lunch and Lilla's hangover has finished although she says she still feels raw and delicate. I send Natalija away to play in her room as I know this is not going to make Lilla happy, what I am about to tell her. I calmly say *that she will leave university and take the dental receptionist vacancy we have in the surgery. She is not mature enough to be unsupervised and she would be better off working. There is no question, no argument. She will do as I say. I am her husband and I know what is best.*

I need to keep her under control as well.

"I hate you, I hate you," she is crying. "I am afraid of the dentist, why would I want to work in a dental surgery?"

I grip her arm and I tell her *she will do as she is told, she is my wife and she does what I say.*

Besides, this is an excellent way to overcome this fear she has. She has already been to register as a patient at my surgery in the summer and I checked her perfect little teeth. Why is she still afraid? I do her check-ups, the hygienist is a lovely woman, the staff are good people and she will be useful if we have foreign visitors as she speaks languages.

She doesn't answer but I already know it and I don't want to hear. She is afraid of me. This makes me sad. I know the other staff are afraid of me too, especially the young dental assistants but for my own wife to be frightened of me is depressing.

She has a responsibility, I continue. She is 18. She is an adult and she has to set an example for Natalija.

In the dental surgery I know she will not get into

trouble.

She married me and made a commitment not just to me but to my little girl, I tell her. Did she think marriage was something she could pick up and put down when the mood took her?

She agreed not only to be with me but to be a mother to Natalija. She can't do that when she is surrounded by all these young people and their bad drunken influences.

"I never would have married you if I thought this is what it would be like!" she screams.

"No wonder your first wife killed herself!"

She then looks horrified as she knows this was the cruellest thing she could say to me.

This angry accusation should make me shake her until her teeth rattle. This should make me do anything to punish her but it stabs a sword into my heart and I leave the room and cry and cry.

I climb into the bed and cry for everything I did and didn't do.

Soon after, Lilla comes in. She sits on the bed and strokes her hand across my face.

"My darling István, I am so sorry. That was a horrible thing to say. It is not true. I know your wife was ill; it was not your fault. I am sure she loved you so much. I was angry and I said it to hurt you," she says as she smoothes my hair. She sighs. "You are right. I will take the reception job."

I say nothing.

She leans over and kisses my eyelids. "I know I am a replacement for her. I feel I can't live up to her. I never feel like you can love me enough. All these photos of her around the apartment and I look at them every day and feel I am not good enough."

"Lilla, my Lilla. I try. Do you want me to put some of the pictures away?" I vowed never to do this but if it helps Lilla I will. I turn over to look at my ice princess sitting so sadly on the bed. I never considered that she would feel second best. I should have thought of it.

"No, no it is okay. It wouldn't change anything. Each time I see her I say sorry for taking her place," she says. I am facing a photo of Kiára as she says this. I pick it up and put it in the drawer next to the bed. I should not have them in the bedroom at least. It is not helping Lilla and it can't be helping my nightmares when Kiára is appearing in the room and I wake up frightened.

"Kiára would be happy you are here to look after me and Natalija," I tell her. "I know she would."

"Sometimes it is too much, too much," she says quietly. I know exactly what she means. I am too much. Too demanding, too controlling, too crazy.

"You could at least have been waiting for me when I arrived home. I had been in America for 2 weeks and you prefer to be out drinking. You hurt me. Your heart is cold, baby." When I think about it, it still burns.

She says nothing. She sits with me and I feel her ghost-like presence on the bed, her cold hands occasionally stroking my face.

She watches over me, this dark angel. She seems to have a different side to the sweet Lilla I saw at the beginning, all innocent and gentle. I sense the volcanic activity moving beneath the surface or maybe it is just a result of my overworked brain. University meant a lot to her and I have made her give it up for entirely selfish and controlling reasons. I am not a good man. I am a jealous control freak and I am worse, much worse than I ever was with Kiára.

HURT

We both know that Lilla is a replacement and however much she tries she can never live up to my first real love. Neither of us wants to admit to it but it is hanging there in empty space, this thought we cannot talk about. It is there when we run out of conversation halfway through dinner. We know the age gap is a problem despite the fact we look good together and I look much younger than I am, there are still all those years when I was living and she was not. She has just left school and I am 20 years into my career. That is a gap we can never fill no matter how much we might love each other. And I am still unclear as to the feeling 'love'. It is so mixed up with passion, obsession and violent jealousy.

We also both know she has to take care of me when I am sick and the responsibility on her is a lot to ask of a teenager who before me had never even dated a man. It would not have been so bad if this wasn't a factor in our lives but that night I was in full blown psychosis must have been so frightening for Lilla. Neither of us had thought through the long-term in this relationship. I married her to possess the spirit of my dead love. She married me because she is young and inexperienced and was flattered that this handsome older man loved her. She obviously didn't have the love she needed in her life either and grabbed at the first promise of it. Only I am not turning out to be the sweet, tender love she needed; I am jealous, sexually aggressive and demanding.

We are both impulsive and stupid and reckless.

We both made a mistake but neither of us is saying so and the difference between us is becoming more of a problem.

Kiára was only 10 years younger than me but this girl is 28 years younger; only 17 years old when I first met her. It is a whole lifetime gap between us. I know a lot of the love is physical. If she didn't look so beautiful, if I didn't look so handsome we would never have even spoken to each other. But we never talk about it. We just know. Even the physical is becoming a problem as well, as at times I am too demanding, too rough. She asks me *please be gentle, I want you but stop biting me, István. I am covered in bites and bruises. I want you to love me.*

I take her to the dental surgery that Monday and speak to the practice manager. I say *Lilla is very mature, she will be ideal.* There is no question. They agree to take Lilla for the reception job. She is so beautiful and her languages will be useful for any visitors. I start to rationalise at least now we can talk about work together, or people we work with.

I don't have any more protests from Lilla. She puts on her dental reception uniform and gets on with her work, learning the computer system fast. She is good with the customers and although some staff are not happy she just got the job because of my status and because she is my wife, no one dares to question my authority. I might not be head of this practice but I have a reputation in the Hungarian dental world as an excellent dentist and surgeon but also as a bully and a tyrant and this I know. But I do not care. They do not know I have been falling apart in my private life. They do not know the aching loneliness which led to my impulsive wedding to Lilla and some of the bitchy girls are gossiping that given how quickly I married her, they think she is probably knocked up.

I just tell everyone that it was love at first sight.

I hear their idiot gossip but I do not care. 'Poor girl, she has no idea what she has gone and done, imagine being married to him. He really does love himself to take someone so young. I bet she has to do things in bed she never even knew existed.'

Well they are right in a way. Poor innocent Lilla crying on her wedding night after I hurt her.

But really, fuck them all. She is my prize, my achievement. The women are bitches and the men are jealous but no one can say anything which hurts me. I do not care what anyone thinks. Lilla is like me in that way; she knows people are talking about her, but she is in her own world as though they don't really exist for her. She also does not care what the other staff say and is not hurt by their stupid remarks.

I find it strange that this girl who is so innocent and sheltered seems to be totally untroubled as to whether people like her or not. It is that same carelessness I have noticed before. She is good with the customers but she really doesn't care about socialising or even saying more than hello to the dental assistants who are just a bit older than her. It is as though she really is living in her own world and I want her to tell me more as I think her family background would contribute to her strange self-sufficiency and coolness. I never told Kiára about my family for a long time and I have been honest with Lilla from the start, telling her that my parents died when I was 20 and I was badly affected. I don't want to hide secrets but she won't open up even though she is so empathic about my bereavements. She genuinely feels for me and understands.

At the end of her first week is 1st November, Mindenszentek or All Saints' Day. Day of the Dead as Kiára called it, after her visits to Mexico. Lilla has to visit her mother and go to the cemetery to lay flowers for her father and it is the first time she has referred to him, so I feel bad that he died. I still sense she really does not want to talk about it, so I travel alone to Pécs with Natalija to be with Kiára. Maybe it is best. I need to talk to her alone without Lilla. I need to explain what I have done taking this girl as her replacement. This physical divide between me and Lilla is the first feeling I have that we are not really connected. That I have forced my way into her heart and dragged her into my life. And the fact her father died explains another reason why she married a much older man; she needed a father figure. How long he's been dead I do not know. I just resolve to try to be kinder to her as I know I have been harsh with my words and my sexual aggression, and this girl is badly in need of love.

In the cemetery in southern Hungary, I sit in the grey gloom by Kiára's grave and I talk and talk asking her to forgive me. I have been having nightmares where she is laughing at me or spitting out harsh words. Sometimes I wake up and she is in the room staring at me with Lilla asleep by my side. She is always in red, the colour I loved on her but which made me so angry like a chemical reaction I never could understand. I wake up in terror as she stands there at night appearing so real while her younger self is peacefully dreaming next to me. Sometimes I cry out which wakes Lilla up and this ghost of my dead love disappears. I have to sleep with some sort of light on as I have had nightmares for as long as I can remember.

Only these are more disturbing because I am sure I actually wake up and see Kiára standing there or sitting on the edge of the bed but it is not comforting because she is looking at me as though she hates me.

In the cemetery I kneel in the cold air next to Kiára's grave.

"Kiára, please forgive me, please. I don't know if I love Lilla. I don't know if it is pure obsession. But it is helping Natalija and I need her but I never forget you. I am with her because she looks like you, you must know that and you know I want you here with me, even just for one day I keep praying you will come back to be with me. Please be happy for me. Please stop haunting me, I am so afraid at night and I love you. I can't understand why you are so angry with me," I say to her grave as the damp November air wraps around me like a shroud and I feel her hands lightly touching my face.

But I do not know if I am imagining this or it is as people believe, the day where the living can connect with the dead. I gaze up towards Heaven but everything is shrouded in mist today and I am praying I am connecting with her and not just imagining it. Either way I am completely lost in this feeling until Natalija's crying snaps me out of this daydream.

"I don't like it here, István, I don't like it," she is wailing. "Apa, want to go home."

She has called me 'daddy' for the first time. She has always called me by my name because that's what Kiára wanted, Natalija to call us by our names not Anya and Apa. And I hate Apa.

"I think we should leave, baby girl," I say scooping her up. I feel her skin next to my cheek and wipe her tears away.

The gloom seems to be wrapping itself around everything. I see it as the spirit of dead souls, sadly returning to earth for that one day they can connect with their loved ones. I can hear crying through the misty air and see some dim shapes further away by the trees. In the distance there are other voices as people lay flowers on graves but it is all sad. Kiára always told me about when she travelled for Day of the Dead in Mexico where everyone danced for 2 days in celebration of their loved ones and didn't weep and sit in gloom. It was like a party, she had told me and she danced on the streets with her friends wearing orange flowers in her hair. They sat in the cemetery while a thousand candles burned and the air was full of smiles and laughter. But then Mexico is much warmer in November than Hungary. And Hungary must be one of the gloomiest nations on earth with our suicides and our suffering and our dark history.

Lilla is already home when we arrive back and it is dark and misty in Budapest too. Lilla does not seem sad, just gentle and sweet but vacant and Natalija clings to her and won't let go and I wonder if I have confused the poor little girl taking her to her real mother's grave when she thinks Lilla is her mother returned from Heaven. I don't know what to say to either of them. What can I say on a day like this; 'Did you have a nice day?'

So I say nothing and the three of us remain in our own worlds.

I feel guilt that I rarely go to Debrecen to visit my parents' graves. If I am there for a meeting or conference I do, but the thought of not being next to Kiára on November 1st is too much and I can't go to both places in a day.

After visiting my love's grave and talking to her, I am still having the nightmares of her in the bedroom watching us sleep. I am aware of how little I can share with Lilla. *What can I say about this?* 'I am having nightmares but I am awake and the dead love who is your image is watching us sleep?'

I am less and less convinced that I love Lilla but I love what she represents which is the image of Kiára and when I am in bed with her it is Kiára I am loving, Kiára I am losing myself in. It ruins the moment and I am angry when Lilla whines, "Please stop; that hurts. Be gentle."

Sometimes cruelly I hurt her more. She wants love and I want sex. She is shocked when in an expensive hotel in Paris I push her against the shower wall under the rainhead shower and have her like I want to. It leads to arguments. She says *she wants to be asked nicely*. I am angry. I didn't have to bring her to this conference, I thought it was a treat for her to see Paris. I tell her Kiára was born in Paris but then I remember that she hated Paris too, always referring to it as dirty and sleazy and not in the least bit romantic.

"Is that why you brought me here?" says Lilla. "Because it is linked with her again? And so you could just have sex with me and hurt me or just so you could think of her when you are with me? What happened to the gentle lover I had?"

I feel the comment *'just so you could think of her when you are with me'* penetrates my bones as she has spoken the absolute truth without realising. She is just upset but that is exactly why I was ever with Lilla, why I married her and wanted to possess her; because I see her as a reincarnation of my dead love and I am convinced she is a young Kiára.

But Lilla is not happy in Paris and says *why can't I ask her if I want to have sex in the bathroom and not the bedroom?*

"Goddamn it, Lilla. Do you want me to ask your permission every night as if you doing me a favour? Are you going to say, 'Not tonight, I have a headache'? You don't have to do much anyway, just lie there like a corpse like you usually do." I am nasty and cruel and I shouldn't say this.

She is hurt and her tears slide down her face and I end up feeling like a monster again. I am not a nice man.

"I love you, I thought you were the most handsome man I had seen, like a film star and now I know you are cruel. You don't love me. You only love sex. You're an animal! Did you hurt her too? Did your hurt your first wife as much as you hurt me? But I love you, I love you, I shouldn't but I do," she says scrunching up in the corner of the shower.

"I love you too, baby but I am your husband and I love sex. I thought you knew that, Lilla. It is the one thing I missed more than anything when I was alone. I love to fuck."

It sounds nasty the way I say it but I am just honest; yes, I love to fuck and I am not having her whining she doesn't feel like it this night or that night or the location is wrong. I am her husband and I call the shots.

"And you are a wonderful fuck, Lilla, you just need to stop being so uptight and you would be even better. Learn some techniques." I reach for the shower gel as the water rains down on us.

She sits on the shower floor weeping and saying *she is not a 'fuck'. She thought I wanted to make love to her, for it to be special.*

I pick her up gently and tell her *I love her more than anything. Yes, I loved her first because she reminded me of Kiára, but I love her and Natalija loves her and I am sorry for hurting her physically but I get swept away in the passion and love I am feeling and I really don't mean to hurt her. When I say 'fuck' I also mean it in the tenderest possible way.*

She looks doubtful as if 'fuck' to her means something nasty.

I am spending most of my spare time comforting her in Paris. She is too afraid to leave the hotel alone when I am in the conference despite speaking excellent French. She says the men follow her down the street. Well what man wouldn't follow someone so lovely? But she is nervous. She is just a girl who has hardly even been out of Budapest and again I am expecting too much.

She is a distraction in Paris when I am trying to work and the conference is demanding with long days. I do love Lilla at times. I have the same feeling I had with Kiára that I will die if she leaves me, maybe I am beginning to love her as much as Kiára or maybe it is pure obsession. Either way I know I need her so desperately that I married her way too early just to keep her. I dragged her out of university and installed her in my dental practice to trap her. I say to her that night, "Promise you will never ever leave me, Lilla. I will die."

"I promise," she tells me and strokes my lips. "I know it is difficult for you with your work and your illness. I'm sorry I don't please you as much as I should."

"You do, just by being with me. I never thought I would love again. You're young too, and I forget that and I expect too much of you, Lilla. I am demanding and I told you to leave university. I am a bully." I lie in the dark ashamed. I think of Lilla dancing in a nightclub with young people her age, laughing and drinking. I stole that from her.

"It's okay; I really like my job. It worked out fine, please don't worry tonight," she says truthfully. Once she started work she didn't whine about being hauled out of university. She just got on with it and it is nice for her to earn money, not that we need it but it is good for her.

I wrap myself in her honeyed skin and she twists her hands in my hair and we sleep entwined as one flesh. Maybe what she never knew she won't miss. Her one university party left her with alcohol poisoning. That is not good.

I decide I will not take her to any conferences again. I need to be alone and concentrate on dentistry. Besides, I don't like to leave Natalija too long with the au pair since we have Lilla now. In conferences I like the hotel bathrooms as it helps me focus on my work and we are always ending up in the bathroom which Lilla says *she doesn't want; it is hard and cold and not loving.*

Goddamn Lilla. She thinks anything other than a bed is forbidden. She has no passion in her soul.

Lilla needs to look after Natalija while I am away. I have not been attending enough conferences over the past 2 years, putting Natalija first who is fretful when left for a few days with an au pair. Last August I had to take her to Munich for 2 weeks just so I could attend a conference and see Natalija in the evening but she cried during the days despite the kind family a friend recommended who looked after her.

Now I have Lilla and when she is not working it is her job to look after Natalija. Lilla has no objection, she loves the little girl. My head is confused as I keep thinking 'our daughter' when Lilla is really young enough to be her sister. She has become her mother. Natalija now thinks the photos of Kiára are Lilla.

So Lilla looks after Natalija when she is not in the dental surgery. The staff know how old she is and how old I am and I think they see me as a predator. I know the women do not like me although they never say anything. I just get on with my day. I don't really care for people's opinions although I am careful how I speak to Lilla in public. I know my words are harsh at times and then I am begging her forgiveness. I make her cry without intending to when we are at home as my jealousy rages out of control and when I find out she has met up with Krisztina and a few university friends she met in the short time she was there and hasn't told me, I go mad.

She has taken Natalija along and as I am putting Natalija to bed, the little girl tells me *Lilla took her to the big streets where there were some boys and a girl and they drank coffee and she had an ice cream and it was exciting.*

I kiss her goodnight and tell her to sleep now.

I go into the living room and ask Lilla *where did she go after leaving work and coming home to relieve the au pair of Natalija. Did she take Natalija out?*

"No. Nowhere," says Lilla innocently twirling her hair and not looking up from her girly magazine.

I wouldn't mind if she told the truth but the fact she lied incenses me. If only she had told me when I arrived home, 'I took Natalija to the downtown and we had ice cream,' I would not be angry even if I found out from Natalija that there were boys there. *Because at least she would have been honest.*

It is her complete lies I get so incensed with as it suggests she is hiding not only something now, but at other times as well. How can I trust her? I wouldn't lie to her.

I grab her cell phone from the sofa and scroll down to a message from Krisztina to meet her and Gábor and Iván. Lilla tries to grab her phone back all the time protesting she didn't go anywhere. I smash the phone on the floor and stamp on it. I grab her wrist and tell her *Natalija told me.* Lilla is afraid and pleads with me to stop *I am jealous of nothing. She went to meet them for coffee and took Natalija but didn't tell me as this is how I react.*

"Now I have no phone," she says. "Why are you like this? I did nothing wrong."

"I'll buy you a new phone, baby but you are not sneaking around while I am working meeting these drunken university idiots. You made your choice. You are a woman now and you behave as you should. They are not what you need in your life, Lilla. It makes me wonder what else you are hiding from me. When you lie to me you destroy my trust in you. You are probably so used to lying, baby."

I drag her to the bedroom and tell her *she needs to show me she loves me. She is wearing red lacy underwear for those boys not for me.*

"It's for you, you bought it for me," she says a tear sliding down her cheek.

"Show me you love me, Lilla," I demand as I push her onto the bed. "Show me." Her kisses are sweet but tentative and I give her orders. I tell her to dig her nails in my back; I want to hurt as I have hurt her. She is a better lover than she was maybe because she is angry about the phone but she is getting more passionate and less shy these days. I am addicted to her but as the addiction of the flesh takes over I don't know if I love her or I just love sex with her. My back burns with her scratches as I reach ecstasy. Now I love her. I caress her beautiful golden skin.

"Why do you hate me so much?" she asks. "Why did you want to marry me if you hate me?

I don't understand, I don't understand you." She strokes my arm, runs her hands through my hair.

I can't answer.

"Your soul is black István, as black as the walls in this dark room," she says.

I look at the room. It is tasteful black. Black walls and lots of mirrors. What is wrong with that?

"Even your bathroom is black," she continues.

What is her problem? It is fucking IKEA and I chose the most tasteful bedroom. What does she want? Girly pink?

"It is classy. Unlike you, Miss Trashy." I turn my back on her. "Bet you want pink fluffy heart lights and flamingoes on the walls too. What are you, a gypsy girl? Was your father a gypsy?"

I realise just as the words come out, I shouldn't say this about her father. I should not be insulting her dead father. I want to take it back but it is too late.

"Don't you dare say that about my father!" she shouts.

She swipes her cat claws across my back and pulls my hair hard. I flip her over and pin her down. There is anger in her eyes for the first time. "Well I hate you too," she says. And I think she means it.

Fragments

I pull her hair and fuck her harder than usual and she doesn't whine or protest just kisses me back harder biting my shoulder. We are feral. I have turned her. *That's better, Lilla. You are starting to understand passion now.*

It doesn't last. She is crying again and I feel an overwhelming tenderness, as if she is my daughter. *My little girl. I hold her and promise her everything. I promise to reshape the moon for her, my heart is damaged and it keeps hurting the one I should love more than anything. I tell her I love her now and forever. I kiss the tears and long to turn them into diamonds in my hands like Dracula in a film I saw once.*

She lets me hold her and asks me, "Please love me István, don't hate me anymore."

We have reached the point of no return. I did not see the sign warning me in 8 languages to turn back now for my own safety as I did once when I was driving through a rocky road next to a mountain in Spain. I have lost myself to this girl. I am drowned.

We fall asleep entwined and I dream and dream.

I am dreaming about my son. He is a beautiful boy with black curls and dark eyes and a lovely trusting smile. Levente, my heir to the throne. He is 2 years old and I hold him in the air with pride.

I wake up next to Lilla. There is no Levente. She has not given me a son. Maybe I can persuade her. It is Natalija's birthday next week. Natalija would like a playmate. Lilla should give me what I want. Surely she knows if I married her it is my right to have a child. She is a selfish girl. I watch her sleeping and feel intense hate looking at her beauty. Then I turn away. I am wrong. This poor girl has given herself to me and I have been cruel. I am the monster.

It snows on Natalija's birthday and Lilla takes her to

the garden swinging her round. I watch through the window and again have an image of Lilla as her older sister. Maybe I am too old for her. But once inside she is Kiára again shaking her long hair loose, taking off the fur coat I bought her. She unwraps Natalija's presents with her but I am not feeling well. I am reminded of how ill Kiára became after she had Natalija and hid it from me, her pain and depression until she tried to kill herself. And I was too wrapped up in my goddamn work to notice. I have relived that time until I am nearly crazy, how I could have saved Kiára if only I had noticed her sliding into depression. I could have saved her.

After Natalija has worn herself out with her new toys, Lilla reads her a story and I can finally go and lie down and curl up in the blackness. Lilla was right, the room is dark but I like it. Lilla comes to find me and playfully squeezes my middle. I can't respond. I am too sad.

"My love, what did I do?" she asks stroking my hair. "My love," she whispers. "Are you sick? What can I do to help?"

She might as well not be there. She can't help me.

I drive us to the dental surgery most days if it is cold unless Lilla is working later, then she walks to work. She is wearing red lipstick and seems more made up than usual and later that morning I see her talking flirtatiously to a new junior dentist, András who started at the practice last week. Usually she is pleasant and polite with staff and customers but I notice a difference in the way she speaks to András and I do not like it one bit.

The tart, I think. *The little tart. Right in front of me too. How would she feel if I did that with other women in her face?*

I am having to sit on the volcano which is ready to explode as I have a big operation to do that morning.

When I come out of surgery, she is on her break and so is he. I find them laughing together in the kitchen over their lunch. I could scream at them. I could do a number of horrible things but I want to remain in control in work. This is not my practice and I am trying to keep my emotions out of the workplace, unlike before. I don't want people talking more than they do already.

I try to contain my emotions when I arrive home that night and hear Natalija and Lilla talking in the kitchen. Natalija is lost in her dinner trying to separate the pasta from the vegetables. She doesn't like the black squid ink pasta Lilla wanted to buy as a novelty. Since she started her cookery course, she wants to buy no end of strange ingredients to make the plates look unusual. But she still can't cook. She told me I would like this pasta as it is jet black, black being my colour. It does look unnatural. I quietly mention to Lilla why she made me so angry earlier.

Lilla says softly *nothing was happening. András is just a nice man. She enjoyed talking to him today, that is all. Nothing more.*

"You will never grow up," I tell her. "You will be too busy tarting with men your own age."

I see the hurt in her eyes but she won't argue in front of Natalija. We are speaking quietly, trying to hide the huge spider web of cracks appearing in our marriage.

"Sometimes I wonder if you agreed to marry me just so you could have a nice place to live and someone to buy you expensive gifts," I say in a low voice. "You would have taken any man who gave you a good offer."

Lilla looks down and she isn't angry but hurt. I know as I say it I am not being rational but I just cannot stop these raging moments of jealousy which make me feel as if I will spontaneously combust.

My self-esteem is bad due to a depressive state I can't shake at the moment. She reaches for my hand and starts to say something but I get up and leave her with the words hanging in the air.

The letters slide to the floor and start to disintegrate like our relationship seems to be. Alphabet soup.

Or maybe I am feeling like everything is disintegrating. Lilla must still love me.

VOLCANO

I am so depressed in the weeks leading up to Christmas I hardly care about anything. Lilla is behaving strangely and is snappy with me and Natalija which I don't understand. I think maybe a holiday would help all of us. The weather is awful right now; really grey and depressing and a gloom settles over the city wrapping the parliament and the Duna River in a death shroud so nothing is visible. Maybe the weather is making Lilla depressed too.

Usually I really don't care about foreign holidays as I get to travel for dental conferences but my shrink has told me I have to take ten days or so somewhere hot since I am not working over the holiday period. I must not attend any work conferences. I have just enough points on my dental licence and I need to relax, he tells me. It is imperative for the sake of my health and this time I decide I will try to follow his advice. I think about Kiára and what she liked. She loved the Canary Islands and I never went with her. It was during the time before we were married and she would disappear into the sun and return to me 2 months later. I look at the pictures in the drawer of one of her favourite places, Lanzarote. I book flights and a lovely 2 bedroomed villa away from the tourist traps on the coast yet still within half an hour of the sea. Natalija will love it.

When I surprise Lilla with the photos and the plane tickets and the picture of our villa, she says, "That looks nice but it is so far. It is two flights, István. Is it a good idea?" She sounds uncertain not full of delight as I expected.

I am fucking mad. I am really busy in work and I thought out where we should go and where she and Natalija would be happy over Christmas so carefully, planning it all and finding the best possible villa to treat them.

Ungrateful little bitch. She never left the country before me and I have taken her to Paris, to Munich and now she has a chance to go somewhere warm to escape cold grey Hungary and she can't gather any enthusiasm together, even if she faked it I would feel better.

"Fuck you, Lilla!" I shout and throw the tickets and photos on the floor. "You are so goddamn ungrateful!"

Natalija repeats the curse and laughs.

I am angry with my daughter now and tell her, "Natalija that is a bad word that only adults use. Not pretty little girls."

Lilla follows me out of the room, "István, what did I do now?"

"Nothing, nothing. Just leave me alone," I tell her climbing into the bed.

"I'm sorry," she says. "It looks nice, it does. I was just thinking it is a long journey for Natalija, that's all." She puffs up the pillows around me but I shut my eyes and want her to leave me alone in my misery tonight. I actually miss Kiára so much I take one of her picture frames and fall asleep clutching it. I know Lilla will see when she comes to bed and it will hurt her but I don't care right now.

The next day, Lilla tries hard. She shows Natalija pictures of the moonscapes of Lanzarote and the villa we will go to and tells her we are making a long trip to the moon. Natalija is excited but I can tell that Lilla is still not feeling enthusiastic. She is definitely faking it.

I even get paranoid and ask her that night *is she faking it in bed too? Who is she thinking of tonight?*

"Why would you even think that?" she asks me. "Why do you think....oh forget it."

She gets out of bed and goes to sleep in the spare

room.

Well she can stay there. I don't know what is wrong with her these days.

I decide that I will show her who is boss around here. After she has packed her bag a week later I carefully remove her contraceptive pills and slide them back into the drawer by the bed. She doesn't stir, her face lost in peaceful sleep.

"You will give me what I want," I whisper. "You will give me my heir to the throne. You will do what I say, baby. And it will be good for you. You need to grow up fast. You married me and you will do as I say."

The next day Lilla is right about the journey anyway. It is fucking far and changing in Madrid and hanging around for the next flight is such a hassle. It takes us 20 hours door to door because of the long wait in Madrid. We should have stayed overnight and taken the second flight the next day. That was stupid of me.

Natalija is tired and fretful and I am not in a good mood, we are not talking much but Lilla takes Natalija and soothes her on the long journey. She is a lovely mother and I feel awful for being cruel to her at times. As we land on the black island, it is dark but warm and the stars hang lower in the sky. I see the moon, as I have in pictures, which is just like the melon slice Kiára used to tell me about. I collect the hire car and drive half an hour inland from the airport away from all the package tourists on the coast. I point at the moon and say to Lilla, "See, baby, I reshaped the moon for you. I told you I would."

She says nothing and the moment is lost forever. *Damn her. How can she not appreciate a moon which is like a silver smile in the sky?* I have never seen a moon like it, only in the pictures Kiára showed to me. This is a small island and the roads are in good condition and empty. Lilla carries Natalija into the villa and wakes her so she can clean her teeth. Natalija is scratchy and irritable but Lilla gently places her in the bedroom with her soft toys and says to sleep, we are in the room next door and leaves the corridor light on.

"This is pretty, István. But I am so tired. Let's go to bed," she says. She has her shower and then I hear her rummaging in her bags for her pills and smile at myself in the mirror as I clean my teeth.

A cobra smile.

"Something wrong?" I ask as I get into bed.

"I swear I put my pill in my bag but I can't find it anywhere. István, I must have left them behind. What am I going to do?"

"Nothing, don't worry," I tell her. "You weren't taking the pill the first weekend you stayed with me and nothing happened."

"But I didn't realise then the risk I was taking and this is 10 days now," she tells me.

"Stop making a big deal out of nothing, baby. I am fucking tired. I just want to fuck and then sleep, okay?" I say as I twist her arms and hurt her.

I tell her *I am a doctor and nothing will happen for only 10 days. She needs to stop being so uptight. If she really loves me she wouldn't be so worried if she had a happy accident.*

I order her to get into bed. "Be a good girl, please me like you always do." She looks sad as I tell her how beautiful she is. She is getting so good at pleasing me. She kneels on the bed in her lovely silk underwear and I kiss her and possess her and tell her I love her.

I think of her fertile young body and in spite of the tiredness of the journey and the open door of the bedroom in case Natalija awakes frightened in the night, I let myself go. I take everything I want from Lilla.

I am so tired I can't move to comfort her when I hear her crying softly.

I sleep.

Natalija is shouting the next morning *Look, there are volcanoes like I said.* We have come to the moon but the sun is shining. The sky is a beautiful shade of blue and the land is jet black, dotted with cacti and red flowers. It is so dramatic but I can't imagine wanting to live somewhere like this. It looks like it hasn't rained for 100 years. Lilla is grouchy. She is angry probably due to thinking she forgot her pill, the poor girl doesn't know it was me and my treacherous heart. I feel a scrap of guilt then think *No I am right. She is my wife. I tell her what is best for us and when, not this girl. If I want a child, then I will have my wish.* Natalija is perfect and she would be everything I wanted if Kiára was still alive but somehow it doesn't seem right not to have one with Lilla.

She is so young and beautiful, she should have a child. She is so good with Natalija.

I take us for breakfast and my miserable ice princess toys with the churros and coffee saying it is making her feel sick. She is complaining about everything these days.

"Oh, Lilla will you stop it and just enjoy yourself. I don't want to hear you whining again. I want to relax for 10 days, is it too much to ask?" I say.

Natalija looks at me in surprise. She never hears me speak to Lilla like this.

Lilla looks like she is about to cry, she quickly leaves the table and runs to the bathroom.

"István, you are mean to her," says Natalija defensively.

"Listen, Natalija. You are having a good time, I am having a nice time. We want to enjoy ourselves and she needs to do the same," I say. "We are sitting outside eating breakfast in December. Isn't it good? It is so warm here."

"I thought the moon would be cold like your heart," she says in such an adult way I know the words have come directly from Lilla. I say nothing. I am not getting into arguments here.

Natalija looks at me silently and then carries on with her churros, dipping them into her gloopy hot chocolate. But I know even this little girl thinks I am cruel towards Lilla.

Lilla comes back to the table and she has been crying, her make-up is smudged around her eyes.

I take her hand. "Are you okay? Did you throw up?"

She nods but can't look at me. "You're right, Lilla. These churros are fatty. I don't know how they can eat this sugary stuff for breakfast. They are making me feel sick too," I say.

"I like it," says Natalija.

We visit César Manrique's house, the artist who built his home into lava bubbles and see beautiful flowering cacti and I know from the photos how much Kiára loved this house and museum and this volcanic island so it is really special for me to see it. I also do feel better with the blue skies and the warmth of the sun. Maybe my shrink was right about taking some winter sun. We take Natalija on a tour of the volcanoes in the Timanfaya National Park and we eat in El Diablo restaurant in the centre of the park which offers panoramic views of the moonscape below. Natalija is loving every minute but Lilla says as they are cooking our meat in the well of the volcanic earth that *El Diablo is a fitting name since I am here*. She speaks some Spanish, having studied it with French to a high level and I know she is referring to me as the Devil. I could grab her arm and twist her wrist viciously under the table for her insolent behaviour, but I will not do this in front of Natalija.

I ignore her and look at the beautiful vista with its untouched sweep of black volcanoes and craters. It is so dramatic.

They serve our dinner and she takes one sip of the wine and says *it tastes horrible, she can't drink that.*

I only ordered the most expensive wine on the menu to please her since we are not driving tonight. We had to take a coach into the park since cars are banned.

I take a drink and it is good wine; it does taste like a volcano but it is a good quality red.

Well she can drink the 99 cents a bottle shit from the supermarket next time.

"Look at the moon!" shouts Natalija. In the dark evening sky the moon is rising like a watermelon slice and the same shade of red. It rises above a volcano and smiles down and then seems to sink again.

I am full of awe. Lilla says *it is an ominous sign, it can only mean bad things.*

Again she is ruining the moment. As Natalija gazes at the moon I reach under the table and cruelly jab my fork into Lilla's leg, not too hard but hard enough to hurt her.

She looks at me and I stare into her eyes with a 'fuck you' look. She isn't angry, she lowers her eyes to her plate and her long eyelashes flutter and a tear slides down her cheek.

I am not even sorry. I carry on eating and Natalija does not notice Lilla as she is gazing open-mouthed at the moon.

I know I have to face the tears when we are alone in our room and I shut the door as Natalija is sleeping well and she knows where we are if she is afraid in the night. Lilla cries and cries and says *she wants to leave me, she can't stand it; why am I so cruel to her?* I don't want to get into arguments so all I do is undress her and I see the cut from my fork on her thigh and I kiss it and put a sticking plaster over the cut. I am a sadist. She is moody but I am cruel and I don't know who starts it at the moment, it just seems to be an incessant loop of hurt. I gently lay her on her back and kiss her and she says, "Please not tonight, István. Please don't."

"You don't get to decide, sweetheart. But I will make it quick if it is easier for you," I tell her.

She won't stop crying and it is such a turn off. I am gentle with her and she cries all the way through even though I press my face to her hair and tell her I love her. I want to tell her *'to shut up, she is ruining my Heavenly moment.'*

I can't even hold her afterwards. I feel there is such a gap between us. The most romantic evening she could hope for in, okay, what was an overpriced tourist restaurant but she has to go and spoil it for me. I turn away from her and sleep.

The next morning Lilla is still sleeping when I wake up. I want to wake her up and do bad things to her but when I see her make up still on her face and streaked with tears, I can't. She must have cried herself to sleep. She is moody on this trip but I feel so full of tenderness and then guilt as I remember last night. *Stabbing her under the table with my fork.* I had drunk 2 glasses of wine but there is no excuse.

I am a terrible man; I am hurting the girl I love.

I get up and fix her breakfast in bed while she sleeps even though I hate it myself, hate the crumbs getting in the sheets.

I have to gently shake her to sit up as I place the tray with juice, croissants and coffee next to her. She is grateful but quiet and I sit and watch her as I drink my coffee. "Darling, I am sorry about your leg. I am a bastard."

"You are," she says. "I think sometimes you wanted someone in your life to hurt and you chose me." She dips her croissant in her coffee but she is not angry, more totally lost and sad. She looks like someone so alone in the world and it hurts me so much that she feels the way she does.

"Look at me, baby," I tell her.

She doesn't.

I gently caress her face and say, "I love you and I am so sorry I hurt you..." I can't say anything else as Natalija leaps onto the bed and says she wants croissants too.

"Here, Natalija, you can have this one. I feel a bit sick, I can't eat two." Lilla gives her the croissant.

I go out of the bedroom to get Natalija some milk and then I sit by myself in the kitchen wondering how far I am going to go down this pathway of pain. Hurting women, controlling them, demanding they do as I say.

Something has gone badly wrong.

We take the wine route cutting through the centre of the island and stop at bodegas. I am interested in how they grow the grapes in this barren land, in neat little semicircles in the ground. I tell Lilla she can taste the wine if she wants as I am driving. She is not happy, more like a sulky teenager. I buy some wine at Stratus, the best bodega on the wine route while Lilla sulks at the bar totally unappreciative of the 6 samples of their best wine complaining it is turning her stomach. I am angry. I want to be sampling the wine but she can't drive so it is not an option. The age gap between us is now appearing like a huge looming crater from the volcanic national park.

She runs out of Stratus. I follow her and she is throwing up outside into some giant cacti and I feel bad then.

"I'm sorry, Lilla. You don't have to drink the wine. You obviously picked up some kind of virus on the flight. Don't worry, baby. I will buy some half bottles to sample back in the villa," I tell her.

"I think I picked up something on the flight, you're right. I don't feel well at all," she says sitting by the side of the road.

The sun is good for me. The white buildings, the black moonscape and the lovely flowering cacti are so different to anywhere I have visited. We have a hired car so I drive us to the west coast to El Golfo through the amazing black moonscape and take Natalija to the beach of Caleta de Famara which is far away from the package tourists. Our villa has a swimming pool just for Lilla as she told me before she loves to swim. She is ungrateful and has the occasional swim, complaining the water is too cold. Natalija splashes around with her flotation bands and is as happy as me.

Fuck Lilla. We have come from somewhere cold and grey to this warm paradise and all she does is sulk and whine.

I am feeling better and I am happy to be here, despite the 4000km distance and two flights from Hungary.

I have given up on being angry with Lilla and I just immerse myself in the warmth of the Canarian sun and play with Natalija, floating in the swimming pool looking up at the infinity blue of the sky.

Lilla is hardly talking. I see her as a sulky, miserable teenage daughter until the nights when I tell her I love her and she fights with me like a wild cat telling me, 'No, I don't want to' and the scratching and biting only make it more intense as I overpower her and laugh at her useless struggling. I tell her *she is my wife and she will do what I tell her, I am not having her saying she is not in the mood tonight or any other night.*

"And if you stop fighting me, I can get it done a lot sooner," I say as if I am performing dental surgery.

"That makes it sound horrible," says Lilla.

"You are making it this way. I thought you loved me. I thought you loved it when I do this," I tell her.

"I do, but I feel strange right now. Oh, just do it already," she says angrily.

I pull her hair back hard and tell her, "Do not speak to me like that, do not give me orders. I am your husband. I decide."

I am hurting her but at times she is making me so mad, I can't help myself. I am sorry about the night in El Diablo restaurant, how I made her cry all night but when she is just sulky I am fucking mad.

My back is covered in claw marks from her nails. When I wake her up and love her just before dawn, she has all the passion of a corpse and just lets me do what I want.

She cries every night quietly when she thinks I am asleep and I hold her and whisper, "Baby, what's wrong? Please tell me, I will do what I can to help you. Are you still feeling unwell? I am sorry if I've been angry with you at times. Do you want to see a doctor?" I know I am forcing her to have sex at times especially now but I see it as my right. She married me. She knows I expect it. I am not going to be sexually frustrated as that will make me even angrier.

But she never answers so I hold her close and hope she will get over whatever it is that is hurting. Or at least talk to me about it.

She goes to a medical centre after I persuade her the Spanish doctors are very thorough and she might as well before we fly home and I ask her when she gets back *is she okay? Is it a virus?*

She doesn't look at me and says as she pours some milk from the fridge *it was just a small virus, nothing to worry about.*

But she still looks so sad.

As we fly home, Natalija sleeps curled up next to me and I whisper into Lilla's hair *that I love her and I am afraid she doesn't love me.* She is crying against the window on the plane.

She says *she loves me more than anything but she feels I am so cruel towards her she can't take it anymore. The sun and my happiness brushed away any communication between us and I haven't talked to her that much in ten days, haven't asked her how she is. As long as I am okay, Natalija is happy, she doesn't matter.*

She bursts into floods of violent tears in her seat making people look at us strangely and I hold her and tell her *I will give her my life, my life Lilla.* She reminds me so much of Kiára like this, both of us afraid the other does not love enough. I haven't learned from my mistakes. I am condemned to repeat them, hurting Lilla like I did with Kiára.

It's not true I haven't asked how she is. I kept asking her to tell me why she was crying, could I help her in any way but she wouldn't tell me what was wrong. I just think she was probably sick with some virus and it has made her feel moody.

These planes are easy places to catch viruses with all the dead air circulating round and round.

When we reach our apartment at midnight she rushes to the bedside cabinet and hunts down her pill and I laugh and tell her *that is not going to work, it is a bit late for those to work after 10 days.*

She turns round and screams, "You did this; you took it out of my bag, didn't you? I hate you! My mother was right. I hate you! I don't want a baby, fuck you!"

She flies at me and scratches my face and I hold her arms to stop her hurting me and she wrestles with me until I calm her down and say, "Lilla, please just have a shower and we will go to bed. You are overreacting and I am really tired. I am treating you to everything I can, and you throw it all back in my face."

She locks herself in the bathroom and I hear her crying in the shower. When she comes out she sits on the bed. The candles flicker on the bedside table lighting up her beautiful face and I reach out and smooth her hair back telling her *I am sorry if I did something or everything to upset her. I am too controlling.*

"I have to tell you something. It isn't your fault, István. I'm sorry. That time I had alcohol poisoning in October, that's when it happened. I threw up my contraceptive pill for a few days. I'm fucking stupid. My moods are messed up."

"Hey, come here," I reach out to her in the dark. "Why didn't you tell me?"

"I don't know, I don't know," she says crying into her hands. "I hate you and I love you and I didn't want this to happen. I kept thinking I was imagining it, I only felt sick in the morning and I couldn't face alcohol and I thought it might go away if I didn't think about it. The doctor in Spain confirmed it. He smiled when he told me. 'Your husband is a lucky man', he said. The doctor thought I would be happy and I cried when he said it. I just wanted it to go away and I put it out of my mind."

I laugh at that. "Where did you think it would go away to?"

I am only teasing her; she sounds like a schoolgirl who got herself knocked up and thinks if she ignores it, nothing will happen.

"Shut up!" she shouts and pulls my hair.

"Hey, come here, baby. Stop stressing. You will be fine, I am here for you. I will look after you. You will have all the help I can give you, every day. There is no need to be afraid. This is great news." I hold her to me tight.

"Not for me it isn't. What a mess," she says crying into the darkness.

I stroke her body and she says, "Please, please don't make me tonight, István."

"Ssh, I won't hurt you, I won't be long," I tell her and despite her tears, her fragile state and the fact she is saying no, I do anyway. She means *no, please don't, I really don't want to*.

I am not a good man. No to me just means I have to comfort her more afterwards. Tell her I love her as she cries.

I always wonder if she would have accepted her situation if it had happened the first weekend we were together, last January when she hadn't started the pill. I wonder if she would have accepted the child more as she had not gone to university then, not seen more of the world and would not be questioning it as she is now. I always wondered long after that if she would have stayed sweet, carried on loving me the same and not become the angry resistant girl she turned into.

If I thought we were not having volcanic love like the fire and passion and hate between me and Kiára, I need not have worried. Since we came back from Lanzarote, all we have done is fight. Lilla seems to have brought back fragments of volcano with her as she has shed the sweetness of our early days and turned into an explosive fiery ball of rage. She hates me, sometimes she loves me but mostly it is angry. She fights me every night, hurting me and I hurt her too. I like it; I like her passion even if it tinged with hatred. It is better than her saying, 'please don't tonight, please just hold me.' But in the days and evenings it is so tiresome. Passion at night is one thing but her sullen and angry alter ego which has emerged is not nice.

I try to be understanding as her hormones are raging out of control and it is not her fault, but I am not used to this side of Lilla. I never knew she could be like this. I thought she would always be sweet and obedient and gentle. When I am tired after work I return home to this angry girl. She is playing with Natalija and I come back and she is moody and snappy with me.

I am happy that she will give me my heir to the throne in July but her terrible mood swings since December really are extreme. She is angry all the time, she is sulky and she hates me as her hormones are in overdrive. She is full of vitriol hating the child already; how could I have ever have thought she was like Kiára when she is the Devil under that sweet angelic front?

Or maybe I am wrong. Maybe I am the Devil; tricking her, hurting her, controlling her and I feel guilt a lot of the time.

I remind her that *she tricked herself, it was her student drink binge that led to this and not me hiding her pills.*

Yes but you hid them anyway, you wanted to trick me.

Well you were so hopeless the first weekend with me, you didn't have a clue. You could have had an accident a year ago since you didn't know what the pill even was. God, Lilla. You are so dumb sometimes I think I married a 14 year old.

And you're a bastard.

I am your husband, you will respect me and don't you dare speak to me like that. It's just as well you're going to have a baby because it might make you grow up.
I hate you.
Good. I hate you too, Lilla.
And she drags her claws across my face. Fuck, I will have a mark tomorrow. Everyone will know.

I bite her hard and suck her blood and we spit and scratch and fight each other into the night.

And so we carry on.

We start arguing all the time. Trying to hide it from Natalija

It always starts when she scowls at me when I return from work and pushes me away when I try to kiss her and ask her how she is feeling. She fights me in bed and we are like wild animals, spitting, biting and scratching. Her claws in my back and me biting her neck and her shouting, "I hate you, I fucking hate you!"

Then her tears afterwards saying *I don't love her* and me trying to comfort her.

I will reshape the moon for her; I will do anything to make her happy. Please stop hating me, Lilla.

She hardly speaks to me in work as February melts into March. She hates me even more.

She says *she is even angrier. If she had to have my goddamn heir to the throne, why now?*

She jabs candles into a birthday cake she is making for me still full of rage even when she is trying to do something to please me. She has already jammed her red roses into a vase and said, "There, watch out for those thorns. Although red is supposed to mean I love you."

"Don't you?" I ask her looking at the roses sadly. It is my goddamn birthday.

Fragments

"I told you I didn't want a child so soon, István and you didn't listen. Now are you satisfied? I am miserable as Hell. I feel sick all the time and I am only fucking 18 years old. I really hate you!"

I stroke her hair pulling her angry young body into me and saying *everything will be okay, I will take real good care of you. I will give you the world Lilla. You will give me a beautiful child and I know you will adore him.*

"Yeah, it's your desire that it's a 'he' as if girls are not enough. I do not want it," she says angrily.

"I would be less angry if I had a daughter like lovely Natalija."

"You'd still be fucking moaning," I say losing my patience again. "Complaining you feel sick, whining on about your clothes getting tight. It is only a few months and it will be over. Get over it, already. And don't forget you made the mistake, throwing up your pill after your university drink binge. It is your own fault."

Then she is crying hysterically saying *I don't love her, I am cruel and she wishes she was dead.*

And I am holding her down on the kitchen floor as she tries to hit me as I am telling her *I will always love her, she is emotional. Let it go, baby, let it go.* She cries into my chest.

"Stop fighting me, Lilla. Please stop fighting me. It is making it worse for you. I'm sorry you feel so bad. It can't be nice for you with what your body is going through, I really have no idea. Just please stop hating me for it."

I eat some of her sickly cake just to stop her crying.

"It's good," I lie. I am worried Natalija heard us fighting but I am not certain so I say nothing as we eat the goddamn cake.

"It's sweet," says Natalija. "István doesn't like it."

Lilla looks at me hurt.

"No, no it's good, really," I say.

She walks out of the room and goes to bed.

"Why did you say that?" I ask Natalija.

She shrugs and says, "You don't like it, I know." And when I look into her dark eyes I know she heard us shouting at each other.

I am so wrapped up in work I do not notice Lilla is drifting away from me; she is more and more unhappy. I am just as bad as her; I think if I just ignore something, it will sort itself out. If I don't make a big deal out of the situation, it will suddenly be fine. I will get home one day and she will be smiling and saying how happy she is.

Towards the middle of March the pain starts to bite from the worst two months for me. The anniversary of Kiára's death is looming and then I know I have made a terrible mistake.

I have done a stupid thing. I have taken on a girl who was the image of my dead love only she was not her. She was sweet and innocent and now she hates me. I know many people would not do what I do and what I did and as she glares at me with hatred as she plays with Natalija I am lost. I love her but I see no sweet girl now, only a girl who despises me. I couldn't bear to throw her out because of Natalija who adores her and because of the child she will have; hopefully she will change her mind and love him. And because underneath all the hatred and anger I feel towards her at times, I look at her and I still love her. Despite all the fighting and fire at night and the scratches and spitting, I know I can't let her go. I just cannot understand why she is like this. I am kinder than I have been before and the hate is still there. I am softer, like clay instead of the hard, unyielding man I was and still am to everyone else but it goes to show sweetness is getting me nowhere.

Or nowhere with this girl.

She is angry about this 'devil child' she has been tricked into having, as she describes him.

Devil boy, devil child. What does that say about me?

I know that was stupid, I should have waited and talked her into it over time instead of rushing her. She is still only 18 and I am the stupid one for rushing everything as if I don't take what I want right now, it will leave me forever.

Then I remind myself it was her mistake in the first place. I just wanted him that's all. She's the one who got drunk and threw up her pill.

Stupid girl. I am giving her everything she never had. Her mother was poor, her father dead and now she has designer clothes, holidays, a beautiful apartment. I have given her a nice place to work in and security for life. She is having the family life she must have only dreamed of having years before I met her. I do my best and this is how she behaves.

And then she does leave me.

No note, no angry words. We didn't argue the day before or the day she left but one day she is in work and I finish later and arrive home and Kata, the au pair says Lilla hasn't arrived back which is strange. Nothing worse than usual and then she is suddenly missing. I am desperate with worry as I immediately sense something is wrong. She is not out drinking with her university friends, she wouldn't because she would have gone home to Natalija and she can't face alcohol at the moment. I just know in my heart when Kata tells me Lilla is not there that something is badly wrong. I am feeling a cold sense of horror creeping over my skin. I call her mother and leave a message on her answerphone, not expecting anything in return.

I call Lilla on her cell phone and I hear it ring, useless and abandoned on the kitchen table. She left it deliberately. I have no idea how I can trace her. When I hear it ring on the table as I try to call her, I feel sick. She never ever goes anywhere without her phone. I rush to the bedroom and look for her passport which is kept next to mine in the wardrobe. It is gone. I have a panic attack there and then. I cannot breathe and have to swallow several klonopin and sit on the sofa trying to think of all the rational reasons as to why she is not here. I can't think of a rational reason for taking her passport. She has left the country. She has gone.

LOSS

The first night without her is Hell. I don't care about her anger and hate. The evening and night without Lilla are so empty. I just want her home. Spitting rage, scowling, screaming; I don't care. I need her whatever venom she would throw my way.

I am desperate with worry. She was angry but what if she was severely depressed. What if she was suicidal and hid it from me? What if she tries to kill herself? It is all my fault, all of this.

I sit up on the sofa and despite my strong medicine I do not sleep at all. I keep staring at my phone, praying for it to ring. It will ring in 10 minutes. Then as 10 minutes go by, I say it in my head again and again and again until I think I am going crazy.

I keep hoping she has gone to a friend's house and I will see her back the next day but I know I am kidding myself. Her passport is missing. I have tried all the numbers on her phone and everyone else I can think of but they know nothing. They are telling me the truth as I have to explain who I am and they all say that they have not seen her for a long time, since before Christmas.

It is 2 days after Lilla has disappeared and I am going out of my mind. I still cannot sleep despite being exhausted in work. I look like Hell. There are black circles under my eyes. I pace around unable to concentrate at home to read even a trashy magazine or watch television.

The other staff in work ask me *am I okay?*

I just brush it off and say *I am having trouble sleeping, I might just go to the doctor and ask for a few sleeping meds.*

They have no idea.

No idea I am already taking enough medicine to

put an African elephant to sleep.

No idea my wife has disappeared and I am going crazy with worry.

I ask my shrink to increase my already high dose of sleeping meds because Lilla has disappeared and for the first time I weep uncontrollably in front of him.

He does not tell me *I told you so, you should never have married her because she reminded you of the Kiára you lost.* He tells me *he will help me all I can and maybe Lilla will be back. Yes, he is sure she will be back.*

He cannot explain her disappearance but I tell him *I know she has probably gone for a termination in another country as her passport is missing.* As I say it, the thought kills me.

That and not knowing where in the world she is. No one has ever done this to me in my life before.

When Kiára travelled away she would always announce where she was going and she always had her cell phone with her. And I knew she would come back. This was before we were married; she never would have done it once I had anchored her and made her mine.

I am given part of the answer by Lilla's mother. She calls me back which is unusual. I know she has to tell me something and asks to meet me in a coffee house. She still does not like me; she makes this very clear. She knows Lilla will have a child, that Lilla doesn't want it.

Lilla said *she would get rid of it but was unable to because of being afraid of me.*

Lilla's mother is very angry that I dragged her out of university but she says I need to help Lilla. She explains what happened to Lilla's father.

He committed suicide by jumping in front of a train when Lilla was 12. He was severely depressed and they were out for the day. Lilla saw everything, saw her father take his own life and stopped speaking for nearly 2 years. She loved her father, Ágnes says.

Lilla is damaged. She has severe post-traumatic stress disorder; she is depersonalised according to the child psychologists who tried to help her but Lilla refused help. Refused to talk. Now Ágnes sees a change in Lilla. She thinks that Lilla is falling apart and she is worried. She thinks Lilla is too young for this child, she is worried sick herself as she does not have any idea where Lilla could be. She admits she wasn't so good with Lilla, she was lost in her own grief for her husband and as Lilla just never spoke she did nothing about it. By the time Lilla began to talk again, they had already drifted apart.

"She is just a girl. She should not be alone like this. You did not do enough and now, God knows where she is," Ágnes says. "God only knows. She could be anywhere. I curse the day she ever met you. You ruined her life."

I pushed her too much. I rushed everything.

"I would do anything, anything if only I could find out where she went," I tell Ágnes.

I only know she could be anywhere as she has taken her passport and her identity card and her bank cards, everything she needs but only very few items of clothing. The beautiful dresses and shoes I bought for her are hanging in the wardrobe discarded, rejected. She has taken the sapphire necklace she wears for special occasions, the first gift I bought for Kiára. Bitch. Then I feel sad. Maybe she took it to remember me when she wears it.

Maybe she will touch the cold glittering sapphires and realise how much I love her and come home.

As I leave the coffee house and Ágnes sitting there, I walk away horribly sad. I know Lilla would have been so disturbed when I had my manic episodes, when I got ill and cut my wrists, when I got depressed. But she was almost better caring for me than when I am okay. Maybe she feels she can help whereas she couldn't help her father.

Ágnes has told me *she still does not like me, she thinks I am controlling, I am ruining Lilla's life but I can at least try to help her.*

"At least now she has a good home life, she has clothes and holidays I could never afford to give her. But she really does not need this child; she is too young to be a mother. She needed to be in university with people her own age."

I am angry to think that Lilla considered a termination and didn't even discuss it with me. If she had, I would have been upset but at least I could have reassured her, she will have all the help possible.

If she has gone to a clinic and got rid of the child she will destroy me. I will hate her forever.

I send email after email just in case Lilla is online. I tell her *whatever she is feeling, even if she can't come home please let me know you are okay. I am desperate with worry.*

Each day, twice a day I check my email and there is nothing. I just hope she reads everything I am writing to her. I hope she knows how desperately I want her home.

For the first week I am cut to pieces; the fragments of my heart lie shattered all over the apartment.

The amber palace I built for her is cracking and splitting down the centre.

Natalija is crying all the time and saying that *mama doesn't love us* and I return home to only the au pair who tells me every single day that she is sure there is an explanation.

"She was probably scared, István," says Kata. "She is only young. She won't stay away forever but I know it must seem like forever to you."

She is saying that to try to make me feel better

whereas really people do not know. No one really knows the dark heart of Lilla, not even me.

I am in despair as each day passes and she does not call; her phone lies useless in the apartment, which is even more cruel as I know she left it deliberately so I cannot call her. I cry all evening for a week. I hardly eat. I even go to church and pray. I do not believe in God but I sit at the back of the catholic church and weep in front of Jesus on his crucifix. I kneel and beg someone to return Lilla; *an angel, a spirit, anyone living or dead, please help me.*

I have tried everyone I know again; the university friends, her doctor, but even her mother says she still hasn't heard from her and she has called her relatives in Eger and no one has had any calls from her. She is 18 and an adult so I doubt the police would do much, they would say she left of her own volition. By Lilla's mother's distress, I know she is truthful. I am catatonic with depression and I have to go into work each day and pretend I am okay.

Then as days turn into weeks, I am angry. I let her into my life and heart and she used me and hurt me and left her stepdaughter and me so callously. Not even one line to say '**I'm sorry but I need some space and I love you both**'. She is the monster. Natalija is crying herself to sleep even when I go and read her favourite stories in English like Lilla does.

I hate her so much I even begin to hope that she is dead; then at least I can grieve over her. I do not know what she has done about the child. I can only think she has done what she said and gone to the clinic and destroyed him.

I don't tell anyone in work. I can't admit what Lilla has done to me. I say *she is ill with bad flu and will need a few weeks off work; she is very sick.*

I am so angry I do something I will regret forever. I want to hurt Lilla really badly. I want to beat her for the pain she has caused me but I feel that I will never get to see her again. Each time I remember it burns. *If only we had talked, if only.* 'If only' spins around my overworked brain night and day and nights are the worst. If I sleep I wake up at 02.30 or 03.00 in the morning and the angst and anger and needles in my chest make me get up and just do something, anything. I go into the kitchen and quietly build the health clinic I was planning out of Lego. It will probably never happen now, but I can't concentrate to read. I get out Natalija's space Lego and try to lose myself in the building blocks, creating fantastical moonscapes and crazy-coloured clinics staffed by smiling Lego astronauts. It is all useless to me now, but it helps and stops me tipping into complete madness in those dark silent hours when everyone else is sleeping and I should be with my Lilla.

The anger continues to burn like a volcano fire and it will not stop. So one Friday, I go to one of those bars in the downtown where travellers go to get drunk. It is rammed full of screeching young Brits and Americans and Australians twenty or twenty five years younger than me swallowing lurid-coloured shots of disgusting drinks. Hateful self-confident drunks who come to Budapest as a cheap watering hole. They stay in the hundreds of hostels scattered throughout the downtown and drink and have sex and cross off another destination on European travels, moving on to Prague or Bucharest or Bratislava or wherever young Westerners can drink and fuck and disrespect the local culture.

I walk in and it is early, around 8 in the evening and everyone is already smashed. The music is too loud and scratches through me like barbed wire being stuffed into my ears. I am not after the drink. I see a girl, a blonde American who is very attractive probably the most attractive girl there, maybe 21 years old and she knows she is beautiful. I do not like blondes as they seem so pale and dull compared to the dark-haired beauties I have always fallen for. I head straight for this roadkill and I chat her up and buy her drinks and she is flattered to have an older, handsome man treat her like a lady and "Not after only one thing unlike the young men here," she says.

Oh, but sweetheart. I am after only one thing. Why do you think I am in this Hellhole in my designer suit? I pay for her violet and blue and unnatural-coloured jelly shots and whatever trash she is throwing down her neck and I tell her *she can come back with me if she wants. I live in a lovely part of town but I have a little girl so we need to be quiet.*

"You guys, I've scored! These Hungarian men are hot," I hear her say above the music as she leaves her travelling companions and grabs her coat and bag.

You stupid drunken slut, I think. Her shallow friends or hostel companions look like they are so wasted with their glazed eyes and floppy bodies they can't remember their own names and in 5 minutes will probably forget she was even there and who she is. These vacant-looking foreigners, as idiotic sober as they are drunk. They disgust me so much. Doesn't this dumb girl realise why I am completely sober and driving us to God knows where for a reason? They have no regard for their safety. I could be anyone. A cobra in a Gucci suit.

Kata, the au pair is waiting for me so I have told this Sofia girl she must wait in my car. I have to see if my daughter is asleep. Really, I need Kata to leave before I take this stupid blonde in. I do not want Kata to know and I also must make sure Natalija is deeply asleep. My mind is clear.

Sofia is merry from drink, more drunk than she had seemed in the bar and this makes me disrespect her even more as she staggers and laughs so I put my hand over her mouth. She is about to walk through the apartment in her shoes so I pull her back to the front door roughly and whisper in her ear, "Take your goddamn shoes off in my house, show some respect, lady."

She laughs as she thinks I am being funny as she reaches down to take off her fuck-me shoes. She doesn't realise I am already hating her. She cannot see my expression but I catch a glimpse of myself in the hallway mirror and I look dark and evil. My eyes are completely black and that is when I know I am dangerous. Kiára told me that look made it appear as though my soul had left my body. I grab Sofia's arm and lead her to the bedroom.

She has condoms although I bought a packet to use on such a slut like her. So she wants it and tears off her clothes and tells me *she wants it hard and fast* so I give it to her, only I am so angry by this point I am really hurting her. She starts crying for me to stop.

I tell her *to shut the Hell up. She wanted it, after all. What did she think she was going to get, milk and cookies?* I laugh and carry on.

And when she is lying broken and weeping into the pillow I grab her clothes and push her into the bathroom and order her to shower and dress and stop that stupid crying. *She was a good fuck*, I tell her. When she is done and she looks so deflated as she emerges from the bathroom and cannot look at me, I grab her by the hair and shove her out of my front door. I have at least had the decency to order a taxi for her to take her to Hostel Rut and Slut or wherever she is staying but she is clearly shaken. I straighten her jacket and tell her *to stop crying, she had a good night and she is a lovely girl*. I stuff 10,000 forints in her bra as I escort her towards the taxi and tell the driver where to take her *never mind her crying. She is drunk and just found out I am a married man.* I give him his generous taxi fare.

10,000 forints. I could have given her a bit more. Well that's all she was worth really.

And I go back to bed and sleep without showering.

The next day I wake up and feel ill. I feel hungover and I didn't drink but I remember the girl and I feel bad. I think I hurt her but I hope she was just too drunk to care. I hope she is okay. I don't really care about her but I wouldn't want her to be too messed up over it. I shower and throw all the sheets in the machine and pick up the condom packet about to throw it away. I change my mind and put it in the bedside drawer.

Later as I arrive home from taking Natalija ice-skating there is a cop car and two of them get out. Either Lilla is dead or this American girl has told them I hurt her. They are polite but I am terrified I will be arrested there and then, snapped into handcuffs in front of my daughter and all the neighbours will be twitching the curtains to look. I feel ill.

They ask *can they come in to talk.*

I say *of course, come in* and I tell Natalija to go in her room and stay there for a bit and I will tell her when the nice men have left.

As they are pleasant and not dragging me straight into the car, I can only think they have come to tell me they have found Lilla's body. I want to throw up. I am shaking. She has killed herself and I have another wife's death on my conscience. Another love I should and could have saved.

The cops are young. They drink my coffee and say *they are investigating an accusation of sexual assault. They don't want to take me to the station as they do not believe the girl. Just another drunk tourist no doubt out for all she can get out of our country. These rich western bitches and bastards. Not content with drinking and fucking and urinating all over our city, they want to screw us if we try to screw them.* They also know of me and my dental reputation as their boss is one of my patients, he sent them to talk to me and he will handle the case personally.

The American girl, Sofia claims I took her to my apartment and forced her to have sex and anally raped her. I say *I am very ashamed to have picked up this girl. My wife is away, we were having some trouble with our marriage and I picked up a drunk American who was clear from the start it was just one night of fun. She wanted sex, my daughter was asleep so we had to be quiet and when I ordered her a taxi and told her I would not be able to meet again she became insulting and said she would go and tell the cops I raped her.*

The cops are sympathetic. "It is disgusting," says the older one. "They come to our country, no respect and then cry rape. They are drunk and having sex all the time. She was completely out of it when she arrived at the police station last night, so drunk she could hardly speak."

"I know I should not have brought her home, I have a little girl. But I never expected this. I am a doctor, a surgeon. I am a good citizen. I hardly drink; I didn't notice how drunk she was until I got her back here. It was only 9 in the evening," I say. "I was worried as afterwards she seemed so out of it so I got a taxi for her to make sure she got back to her hostel safely. I had no idea she would be so vindictive. I made it clear I was married when I spoke to her in the bar."

The officers nod.

I place 600,000 forints on the table. "We all know how treacherous women can be," I say. "I hope this won't go any further."

"You can be sure of that, sir. We know you are a good citizen. We just had to follow up our enquiries. But it is not necessary to come to the station with us. I think our boss will want to close this case right away," says the older one scooping the money into his pockets. "The whores who come here for cheap drink and then try to pin rape on us. They make me sick, these bitches."

The second one agrees, shaking his head. "I'd like to give them a good slapping myself then they really would have something to complain about. But Hell, who are they going to complain to?" and he laughs in a nasty way. "We're not listening."

As I say goodbye to the policemen who say they are sorry to have troubled me, I am sick to my stomach. I go and throw up and throw up until nothing is left. Because I am sure that I didn't rape that girl. We were having sex, it did get rough and I did hurt her a little but no way did I rape her. Even down to the anal sex. I was sober. I know she said she liked it before we got into bed. She was stripping her clothes off, she was up for it but I do remember her shouting, "Stop, that hurts."

My memory is hazy.

But I am sick at what I have become and how serious this could have been if the girl wasn't just a drunk American tourist. What if I'd picked up a Hungarian woman who happened to be a lawyer or a doctor, someone of influence? I could end up in prison. I am a bad man. I don't mean to cause such suffering and I do. No wonder Lilla left me. Have I hurt her like this and how many times?

I remember her crying so many times; on our wedding night, in the hotel in Paris, in Lanzarote and I remember her asking me *to stop, or be gentle* and I never listened. And I remember her asking tearfully *did I marry her just to have someone to be cruel to, someone to hurt every night?*

I am a disgrace. I put my head in my hands and think of what I have turned into.

The senior cop who was investigating the American girl's case calls me on my cell phone the next day. He is my dental patient. He says *he hopes I didn't suffer too much distress when the cops came to the house.*

"After all, we know what these tourist sluts are like. I've seen so many in my time. And they usually only speak English and go on drinking binges around Budapest, Prague, anywhere cheap. They are asking for it, the men and the women. I am sorry for the trouble, Doktor Úr," he says.

"No problem," I say. "But I will stay away from sex mad young tourists in future."

"Hey a man's gotta eat, you know what I am saying? After all, your wife is away so we all have needs," he barks a laugh. "Nothing wrong with a bit of takeaway."

I feel like I am going to throw up again. I end the conversation quickly and run and heave over the toilet bowl although I have not eaten since God knows when. Natalija is standing in the bathroom doorway. "Are you sick, István?" she says. "Please don't die and leave me." Her dark eyes are sad, as if she understands something very bad is happening. How can she know, she is only four years old?

She sits beside me and strokes my face. "It's okay, it's okay," she says.

My darling little girl. I never want you to grow up and experience the horrors of this world.

You would never love me if you knew what I was really like.

After this I resolve to let her go. *Lilla, my darling Lilla. Did you leave me because of the monster I have become?*

I stop looking for her. I am too busy taking care of Natalija. I cannot get inside the head of this 18 year old who gave me what I wanted and disappeared. How could she leave even if she hated me? How could she leave Natalija? And if she really needed to go, could she not have talked or just sent an email. Just a few words. 'I need some time'. Anything, something. Not this. This is Hell.

She has destroyed me. I really begin to think that she might be dead but why did she have to take my son away? She could have left in July, after having him and never seen any of us again. I would hate her and I would grieve but I would be prepared. I was not prepared for this and to do it at the cruellest time possible, the worst time of year for me is unforgiveable. I go to Kiára's grave on the anniversary of her death and weep into the stone begging her forgiveness.

"I only took Lilla because she was the image of you. I messed up, my love, I messed up. I would do anything for her to come home, I don't care what I have to do but I don't know how I can find her. Please help me, Kiára. I thought part of you was living on in her. I thought she was your spirit."

I cry for hours on that warm April day. I have had to leave Natalija in Budapest. She can't see me like this. And I tell my love everything as I sit by the grave that day, I tell her about the blonde American I feel sorry for now. *I went out to hurt a girl, but I didn't mean to really hurt her, only a little. Really, I didn't.*

I carry on in a daze. I go back to the grey mist in front of my eyes. I am a robot. I am existing and this is worse than before. If I had never met Lilla, I would still be seeking Kiára's image in someone else and there would still be hope. Now there is none. This girl has crushed me and my hope, maybe for good.

I know without Natalija I would jump into the

Duna River like Kiára did. I want to die so badly but I have to be there to comfort my little girl who has lost her mother again. I cannot offer her words of reassurance, I can only say that Lilla loved her very much and she left because of me, not her. I cannot tell Natalija that everything will be okay, that Lilla is coming back because I doubt that she will ever come back now.

I found Kiára again and she turned into a demon and now I have lost her forever. My heart physically burns. How could she? How could she? How could she?

And I have flashbacks of the American girl who wanted everything and then said I raped her. I don't think I did but now I am beginning to question this. Did I carry on when she told me not to? I know I wanted to hurt a girl, as I wanted to beat the Hell out of Lilla.

I am a sick man. And maybe I only got away with it because the whole country is full of bribery and corruption and cops who hate tourists and men like me who must obviously hate women.

I will never go out looking for sex again.

At times I hold Natalija and cry into her beautiful face and think *please never fall in love with a man like me, my angel.*

I hold her to me and she says, "Please don't cry, don't cry. Mama was bad. She hurt you."

"Yes, she hurt me but I think I must have hurt her too," I say. "Love hurts, baby. Love really hurts."

I have nightmares all the time since she left. I even feel the weight of Kiára herself sitting on my bed and I am sure I open my eyes and she is looking at me with hatred, in her red wedding dress. Sometimes she just looks at me and other times she is laughing and at times she is saying, "I died because of you. You are responsible. You let me die. You hurt me, you didn't care and now you are a complete monster. Look at what you have turned into. You are a horrible man. No wonder Lilla left you."

I am screaming, "No, no! I loved you and it broke my heart when you died. I should have done more to help you but I loved you more than life itself. Kiára! Please forgive me, please!"

I shout so much Natalija comes running in climbing on the bed and saying, "István, what's wrong? Who hurt you?" She snaps on the nightlight and I have to leave it on every night after this.

Other times I have nightmares about Sofia crying and telling me, "You raped me and bribed the police to stay quiet".

"I didn't mean to hurt you, I didn't mean to. I thought we were having sex."

But I do not dream of Lilla. I am beginning to think that Lilla is my dead love which is why I am not dreaming of her or more like I am dreaming of an older version of her, my real love. Kiára is telling me in my nightmares that I hurt Lilla even in one dream telling me *she came back to earth for me and this is how I treat her. Now I am just a girl in a girl's body and you are cruel, you are horribly cruel.*

I am losing my fucking mind.

It is this dark bedroom. It does not help. Lilla was right; it is a bit too dark even with the nightlight I always leave on. I take the duvet and sleep in the living room with a brighter light on but I still have nightmares.

DEMON

It is three weeks after her disappearance when Lilla, more beautiful than I remembered her, returns. As she stands in the doorway my first thought is I want to hit her so hard she falls over and then slam the door. But I look at the girl who looks more like my lost love than ever and she sinks to the floor. It feels like three years since she was last here, not three weeks. She wraps her arms around my ankles and begs me to take her in and tells me to kill her for hurting me so much.

"I couldn't kill Levente, I couldn't do it. I thought I would and I couldn't go through with it. Please forgive me, please let me come home," she says and I scoop her up and the tears are falling down her face.

I still cannot pity her after what she put me through.

"Tell you what, Lilla, why don't you just have the child and then go. I mean nothing to you so that is what you can do. I would give you money and you can leave for good. I thought you already had. I thought you were dead." I am full of conflicting emotions, wanting to throw her out and wanting to hold her to me tight and never let her go. I remember saying a similar statement to Kiára once, that if she didn't love me she could leave the child with me and go. I feel awful as I have just said more or less the same thing to Lilla.

"Please forgive me, I will die if you don't let me in," she says as she clings to me and won't let go and I inhale her cloud of Coco Chanel perfume and grow weaker. My resolve cracks and splinters like my personality.

Kiára, let her back in. You love her. Don't let her go.

I look at her and I can only see my long lost love crying and begging me and my heart will not let me throw her out and I pick her up and carry her in. She is carrying a small shoulder bag and that is it. It is Kiára I see, not Lilla. "Levente is still here then despite what you went away to do," I say.

I hold her tighter. Poor girl, she's tiny no wonder it hardly shows. I wish she would eat more.

She tells me *she disappeared to have a termination but couldn't go through with it.*

I am split down the centre. I want to beat her for what she has done but then I am so grateful to see her again I can't stay angry, I just want her back and no doubt I am responsible as I must have been so cruel at times. I shouldn't take her back; I am beginning to feel that we are very bad for each other. My head is screaming to throw her out but my stupid heart will not. I tell her *to just come in, please just come back.*

Natalija is angry and refuses to see her. She stands in her doorway her face full of hurt rage and then she slams her bedroom door.

"Baby where did you go? You broke my heart into fragments, you broke Natalija's heart. If you weren't so damn beautiful I would have screamed at you to leave but I can't. I see you and I see her," I tell her. I carry her into the living room and place my Lilla on the sofa gently.

"I was in Vienna. I have a friend at university there. I had to think about everything."

You selfish hateful little bitch. And now you think you can just come back?

"With a man, Lilla? Who with?"

"Alone, I was alone. Just me and Anna in her student apartment. You can call her. I needed to think. I didn't cheat on you István, I swear."

"I scrolled down every fucking number on your phone and there was no Anna," I tell her.

Lying little bitch.

"Because I deleted her number from my phone. I

wrote it down because I knew you would call and Anna is not a good liar," she says. "If you don't believe me, call her."

Oh but you are a good liar, Lilla.

"István, I swear on my life I did not cheat. I just needed time alone to think," she says her dark eyes full of sadness.

You did. You promised you would never leave me. You broke me. Your treacherous heart.

Natalija comes into the living room. "I hate you, mama. I thought you left because of me. I hate you!" she screams.

"Please, forgive me, Natalija. I needed time," Lilla pleads and holds her arms out to the girl.

"I thought you left me, you died and left me! Why? István was crying," and Natalija sits on the sofa and glares at Lilla. Lilla tries to go to her. She goes to the little girl and tries to hold her. At first Natalija fights her shouting, "I hate you, I hate you, you hurt István!"

Then she lets herself be held and buries her face in Lilla's hair and howls.

"I promise you I thought of you every day, I am so sorry, Natalija. I was so wrong. I was feeling bad and I had to go away but I promise you it was not because of you," she kisses Natalija's face and swears to make it up to her every single day.

Natalija asks suddenly, "Did you kill my brother, is that why you left?"

Lilla looks shocked and can't answer. I pick up Natalija and take her out of the room.

"Your brother is not dead Natalija but she loves you more than him," I tell her. I shouldn't say this but I don't know what else to say to the little girl. She looks at me with those dark eyes and just says *she is glad about that.*

I ask Natalija *please can she give us a bit of time then we can play, anything she wants; go and dig out*

those favourite toys and we will play with you.
Reluctantly, she starts to look through her boxes.

I go back to Lilla sitting angelic on the sofa.

You demon, one touch from you and everyone is okay. You just walk back in and think it is all okay.

My beautiful, beautiful love with your heart of thorns. I hate you so much. You will never get my forgiveness. And you left because of me, because you cared nothing for my heart and what it would do to me.

"Why didn't you even call me, Lilla? You even left your phone here. You could have just called us and said you needed time, anything would have been better than what we have been going through. Three weeks, I was out of my mind. I would have gone crazy after a few days but 3 weeks and not knowing where you were, whether you were dead or alive and you never even called. Do you know what you did to me, to Natalija, to your mother as well? She was distraught."

"I am so, so sorry. My head was messed up. I had to think alone. And you are wrong about my mother. She never loved me. She told me once."

"Did you even read your fucking emails?" I say.

"All of them," she says looking at me with such sadness.

"And you couldn't even send one word to say you were okay? That you loved me? That you weren't dead, just anything, Lilla. Anything!"

"I am so sorry," she says looking down. "I am so sorry."

I should have taken her passport like I did with Kiára. I should have. I will never trust her again.

I hold Lilla and she tells me *she went to the clinic for the termination because her mother told her she was ruining her life. Then she couldn't do it, she ran out of the waiting room of the clinic, to her friend in Vienna to think. She hated her mother after that and her mother told her she never wanted to see her again. Lilla hopes I can forgive her for what she did.*

So the lying bitch Ágnes took her for a termination. She knew about that. But I know she didn't know where Lilla ran away to after the clinic. I want scream at Lilla that minute but the genuine remorse in her words and the tears which fall down her face are heartfelt. She has been damaged in her life and I think I have expected too much too soon with this girl. God, she is not even 19 years old and I am 47. Poor Lilla. I drove her away. Her mother doesn't love her. Her father is dead and I ruin her life even more.

Then I feel rage again. "Why didn't you talk to me, Lilla. Why didn't you tell me how bad you felt? Do you know how little I slept for the month you were away? Do you? How do you think I could work properly on nightmares and hardly any food? Do you have any fucking idea?"

"I am so sorry, I was stupid, I really hate myself for what I did," she says.

If she had only talked and I could have maybe persuaded her to stay. She could have talked about her fears. But talking is not something we have been good at.

But she betrayed me and killed fragments of my heart.

And she left me so broken, more than anyone ever did in my life. She broke my goddamn heart and Natalija's too.

I tell her since she has been away I cheated on her with a hot young blonde in our marital bed. But then I threw her out like garbage.

"István why are you telling me this?" she says. She wipes away the tears running down her face.

"Why would you cheat on me like that?"

I look at the sapphire necklace lighting up Lilla and the stones are so beautiful in the light in contrast to this ugly reunion of desperate obsessed me and fucked up damaged Lilla.

"Because I thought you had gone forever so I fucked someone else and God only knows how many men you have had. I am being honest because you broke my heart so I had every right to cheat as I never thought I would see your goddamn face again," I tell her. It feels good to tell her that. It feels good I hurt her because it is nothing compared to what she put me through. But at least I am honest and I do not even know if this angel or demon is telling the truth half the time.

"Was she good, was she better than me?" she says.

"No, I didn't care for her. And I did use condoms. I had to eat, Lilla. A man has to get take out when he is hungry," I say nastily.

She puts her head on her knees and curls up and sobs uncontrollably. I watch her, enjoying her pain for a minute.

But I can't make her suffer. The poor girl is pregnant and I am gloating over cheating in our bed. I am a sadist. I am not fit to be with this beautiful girl.

I am holding her, telling her I was dying without her. *I only love you, Lilla.*

"You cheated on me, you cheated in our bed," says Lilla tears running down her face. "How could you?"

"And you left me and never even thought to call just to say you were okay. Even if you just said you needed a bit of time alone, even that," I say full of pain. "I would never have cheated if I thought you would return but I thought you had gone forever. I didn't even know if you were dead. How could you do that to me?"

We sit in silence in our own worlds of heartache and obsession and love and hate. How can we do this to each other? Why do we hurt each other so much?

I want to put her straight back in my bed but my

angry cold hurt will not let me. I tell her *to go and sleep in the spare room. I need time to think. I do not know if I want her next to me.*

She cries as she arranges herself and her things in the spare room.

I lock my door that night. I am not having her sliding under the covers as my body is weak and I will end up with her. I want her but my pride will not let me. *She fucking broke me.*

No one does that to me.

No one has ever done that to me.

It can't last, I need physical attention whether we hate each other or not. Since she is here again, I put her back in my room the following night. I still want her, goddamn demon.

"I am here to help you, Lilla," I tell her for the hundreth time. Lilla has gone silent. "I know how much your father's death would affect you. My parents died in a car crash when I was 20. I can understand some of how you feel. But please stop hating me. I am a monster but I am trying. I am trying." I take her in my arms and kiss her hair.

"You're not a monster," Lilla says into my neck. "My father, he...." and she cries and cannot say anymore. I think this is the first evening and night we are not hating each other for a long time, when she shows passion which is more love than hate. She lets me hold her before she sleeps. Usually she moves away from me to sleep and only ends up in my arms later in her unconscious world.

She kisses me with all the sweetness of the first time and my flesh is weak. I wake up in her honeyed limbs with her beautiful face.

Each night as I watch her sleep, I want to drive a stake through her heart. She is the monster not me. I know we could be finished. However long or however many years we go on is up to me. But I know as I look at her sleep, she has a heart so jagged she is capable of anything. I cannot trust that she will come back and she won't disappear again. I have hidden her passport but I can't hide her identity card as she needs to carry it with her by law. She could travel away with that alone. But I know hiding her passport is only symbolic as I have already left her in my head. It is only my stupid heart and body which still cry out for this girl. She opens her eyes as she feels me stroke her hair and she whispers, "My love."

I hate you, I hate you, I think.

She runs her hands through my hair and tells me *she loves me, she missed me so much, missed this so much.*

Fucking missed me. Well I missed fucking you, baby and I think that is all right now. My love for you is dead. I could fuck you into eternity but I don't love you. And you nearly murdered my child, Kiára would never have done that. You left me at the worst time, the time of my saddest moment of the year and I thought you had gone for good. Not a word, not a phone call. I had resigned myself to never seeing you, never fucking you again.

I roll over and look at the picture of Kiára next to the bed. My one and only love. Not this demon next to me. *My love, why did I let you die? I let you down. Why am I with this false love who broke me at my weakest? This demon girl.*

Be careful what you wish for. It was in a fortune cookie Kiára had once and I think how right it is. I longed for my dead love to appear in someone else. I searched and found her and she was hollow and empty. When she disappeared I longed for her to come back and she did and now I realise I hate her and we are living on borrowed time. Natalija has forgiven her but I can't. I have been dreaming about my son, the Levente she will give me and I hate this heartless woman or girl or devil or whatever she is for destroying my dream; it is not sweet any longer. Levente may still be there but she broke my heart by running away and I thought she would never return.

The demon snakes a lovely hand over my back and I shove her hard and pin her down. I must be hurting her but she laughs. This time I bite her shoulder and she just sighs and lets me. I scratch at her skin and she lets me do everything I want as I take out all my anger and hate and she just says, "Do what you want. Hurt me, I deserve it. I still wonder if I should have got rid of the child, but it's too late now." She says it so carelessly I am volcanic with anger. I want to beat her for saying that but I would not do that to her because I can't hurt my son. But I want to; her comment burns through my brain.

You say that now, after what you did? Like a small mistake in your life to destroy a living being? What an unfeeling bitch you are.

"You do deserve to be punished, Lilla. You do. And you are heartless talking about our child as if he is a piece if garbage to be got rid of, just hoovered out of your insides. If you ever leave me again I will hunt you down and I will make you fucking pay for the rest of your life," I say.

She laughs again as if I am just talking like this in the bedroom. I am deadly serious.

I will kill us both.

Then I look into those eyes and I kiss her and let myself drown. *God, Lilla what spell did you cast on me because I want your body night and day. I should have not let you in and now you could break me again.*

"I can never trust you now, I can never forgive you. You promised me you would never leave and you lied. You broke my heart and I can't forget that."

"István, please let me explain..." she touches my face. I have heard it all before. The *forgive me* and *I'm sorry.* I am her husband and she has made me ill with her behaviour. I scratch her hard and pull her hair and she doesn't protest. I hurt her more than I did on our wedding night and she says nothing, she takes the pain I give her, lets me do everything I want and when I bite her neck so hard and suck her sweet blood, she just sighs and runs her hands through my hair.

She makes me sick. But her body is like honey and wraps around me in the same way. I am caught.

It is destroying me as I return each day and Lilla is in the apartment. I am always expecting her to have gone. She has returned to work in the dental surgery as if nothing happened and shrugs when people ask about her *is she feeling better? They didn't know she was going to have a child; she is so slim she hardly shows even now. Is she happy?*

She shrugs again.

She is not.

Is Lilla okay? Is she still ill? They ask me. *Isn't she happy about the baby?*

She is fine. She has just not been well, I tell them. I want everyone to leave us the Hell alone.

She finishes at different times to me and there is always that dread I have when I unlock the door and expect to find an empty apartment. I cannot shake this feeling.

I begin to wish she had never come back. I begin to wish I had never met her that January day when the world seemed soft and beautiful and the sunlight split through the trees.

I slide deeper into my depression spending the evenings and weekends in bed. All I can think of is Kiára. Lilla cares for me. She does her best but she cannot reach me. She tells me she loves me so much. Yet she left me in March for 3 weeks with no word and seems so unaffected. *I thought I would kill you,*

Lilla if you had killed Levente, the son I was dreaming of. You could have had the child and then left us all but the torment you put me through by not talking was Hell. You are depersonalised, damaged, unable to feel. An ice queen but a demon. I hope you will be better with our son.

Even when I return from work one day, she is with some young twenty-something boy chatting on the sofa. All I do is shut the door and go to the kitchen. I don't even feel anything. I just call after him, "Close the door when you leave and don't come back."

Lilla comes after me in her dressing gown. She tries to touch me and I shove her away.

"Lilla, I don't want to hear a word. But I would prefer you stayed for Natalija. If it was just me, I would ask you to leave once you have Levente. I don't love you and I don't even care about your infidelity." I drink my coffee and stare at the wall.

Of course I fucking love her and finding her sitting in a dressing gown as if in the afterglow of sex fucking rips out my heart. But I do not want her to see how much she is hurting me.

"It won't happen again," she tells me. "I promise. And nothing did happen, he is a friend."

"Good," I say. "Because if I find you in my apartment with a man again I will beat you with my belt once you have had our son and I have never hit a woman in my whole life. Cheat if you want, but not in my goddamn bed."

I walk out and gather up the bedclothes. I throw the sheets in the laundry. She watches me hurt.

"Why are you doing this?" she asks me. "I would never......I didn't, I swear on my life."

Then I push her into the shower and follow her in, soaping away her infidelity real or imagined, as I am convinced she is a cheat and a liar. She protests nothing happened then I am having her hard against the tiled wall. She closes her eyes. *Where are you, Lilla? Are you thinking of someone else in your ecstasy? You cheat when you have my child inside you? What demon does that? Or do I still please you enough?* She has a body to die for, the face of the loveliest woman on earth and a heart of fucking ice. *Look at me*, I tell her. I gently stroke her hair but she pushes my hand away and looks at me and tells me to hurt her. She wants me and only me if just for that moment. She bites into my shoulder hard making me bleed. I like the pain, it takes away the pain in my heart.

You beautiful demon. But I can't hurt you too much, not with my son inside you. I can only bite your treacherous throat. Maybe that's why you want me to hurt you. You still want to get rid of Levente and then you could blame me.

"István, I promise you, I didn't cheat on you," she tells me all night. "I swear, he is a friend of Krisztina's and I asked him to call for coffee. I am lonely."

But I open my eyes and look into hers and she smiles at me and I think she did. I think she cheated in the goddamn shower to get me back for cheating when she ran away. She did fucking cheat, I know it.

Like me and Kiára, our world has shut out everyone else. We only exist with each other but it is not so sweet now, there is no passionate obsession. Just the anger, the hurt betrayal I feel all the time. The feeling I can never trust this girl again.

So we carry on. We connect physically. I make sure she has plenty of that so she won't go looking for it elsewhere. We don't speak; just sometimes I see her playing with Natalija I see the girl I once fell in love with who reminded me of my love of my life. But she was not and will never be her. She smashed my heart into fragments, she was careless, and lied. I know I am no saint. I was too demanding, too controlling but I didn't deserve what she did to me.

When people see us they say what a beautiful family we are. We are beautiful but my hate for her is bubbling under the surface and her careless disregard for me is evident when we are alone. I think I preferred it when she hated me. I just lose myself in her honey sweet body and taste her hair and tears and I can travel back in time to the girl I loved, the Lilla who was so sweet and gentle and good. Each morning we wake up entwined and then go our separate ways.

Then the full force of her careless heart stabs me again. Like a delayed reaction and I shake her and scream, "I loved you and if you didn't want Levente you could have him and leave him with me and then have left. You left me then you came back when I was getting over it and ripped me open again and then you cheated on me. Why, Lilla? Why? Am I an old man to you? Am I unloveable?"

I shake her and she cries, "I am so sorry. I am sorry for everything. I ran away because I was messed up, I came back because I loved you but I never ever cheated. I wanted to, I wanted to hurt you but I can't because I couldn't go with anyone else. You are the most beautiful man in the world to me but you make me feel like trash! You hurt me. You married me because I am like her, and I can never live up to her. I look at her photos all round this goddamn apartment and there are none of me. None! I wouldn't be here if she was still alive!"

And we collapse on the floor both crying alone. We hurt and we get hurt. We are so bad for each other.

"I loved you, Lilla, I loved you. You don't realise what you did to me when you shut down on me when we were in Lanzarote and we returned and you were horrible and then one day you left, no note, no nothing and you just come back here into my life and my heart and I find you here with a young man. You were in a dressing gown."

"I had just showered. He was my friend, he arrived early for coffee," she says. "He knows I am married to you; how jealous and controlling you are. How you would hurt any man who touched me. For God's sake, I am having your child in July, how could I cheat?"

"And I bet that is the only reason you didn't cheat." I cannot trust her.

"If you hate me so much why don't you divorce me?" she shouts through her angry tears.

"Because I love you, Lilla, I still fucking love you. I wanted to be with you forever and you promised me that only last July at our wedding. You promised," I say.

She turns me into a child myself, begging, pleading, crying for her love.

She falls into my arms and holds me and *she is never letting go, she is sorry. Her emotions are fucked up because of what happened to her father*, she says. She never really talked about it with anyone. She just closed down.

"You forget, István. I am only 19 years old. You fucking forget. I am only just an adult and you keep expecting too much. I try and try and now my body is full of emotions I just can't really connect with and I am so messed up," she says.

Oh Lilla you are so right when you say that. I keep treating you as an adult. You are still really a girl. I am unfair on you. No wonder you ran away. You hurt me more than anyone has ever done in my life but I can see that you are a lonely, damaged and frightened young girl.

And the worst thing is that you are afraid of me, your husband. I feel awful knowing that. You don't say it but you don't need to. I am a bully. A demanding tyrant who wants to possess your soul. Someone who physically and mentally hurts you.

I am hospitalised again in early June. The stress and depression of Lilla disappearing in March and then returning in April as though Kiára had risen from her grave has messed with my head and has sent me straight back to the psyche ward.

Lilla is sitting by the bed and telling me *it is all her fault, all her fault.*

I know I have to get out of here in the next week. I can't take time off work. Lilla has told them I have flu. I hold her hand. We are beyond words. I have to forgive her.

I squeeze her hand and tell her, "Please never leave me again, I will die. I can forgive you now, Lilla."

I will forgive you for what you did, but you broke me. You are just a girl and destroyed me and I thought I was King. I was wrong. You are more powerful than me Lilla.

Lilla, we can make it okay again. I am staring at the balloons swaying gently on the end of the bed. Natalija brought them again; she thinks a few balloons will help my illness. Cheer me up.

"Do you even know what day it is?" Lilla looks at me with such pain.

"I think it is Tuesday or Wednesday, I don't know, I don't really care," I say.

"My birthday. My birthday and you forgot. Natalija remembered but you didn't," she says.

"I am ill, baby but I will make it up to you; we will get you anything you want. We'll go out and celebrate as soon as I get out of here," I tell her.

She looks at her hands and the cold diamond promising eternity.

"Please Lilla. You promised me everything a year ago, please understand what you did to me which is why I am lying in this hospital. And think about what you would like for your birthday."

"I will try, István. You sleep now."

I am falling asleep. They have given me stronger meds and she is left alone by the bedside.

I can't even remember what she promised me.

I am sicker than I have ever been in my life. I am unable to function and Lilla has to care for me. It is the time she is gentle, she strokes my hair, tells me she loves me. She knows this breakdown is her fault and she tells me so as I drift away to sleep. She asks me for forgiveness but I am too tired to answer.

I lose a lot of time. I have to be honest with the dental surgery. It is not the time of year to get flu. I speak to Linda, the practice manager and she is sympathetic. She thought I was moody and difficult, she had no idea I was struggling to hide my illness. She has an uncle who is a lawyer and bipolar so she is sympathetic. She says *I am such an excellent dentist and surgeon, there was no hint of it in work. I must make sure I am well before I return.* I know I can trust Linda to keep it confidential. No one else must ever know. I do not tell her the trigger for my sickness this time. I do not tell her what Lilla did to me.

When I am out of hospital, I remember my Lego clinic I made during my mania last Summer and all the extras of space Lego I started adding last month when I was going out of my mind when Lilla was away. I get it down from the top shelf of the wardrobe and I place it on the kitchen table sadly. It will not happen but I can't face taking it apart since I put it together with such surgical precision. It has become a mismatch of shapes and colours and incongruous moonscapes and astronauts as I was half-asleep, half-awake when I was snapping blocks onto it.

I am too ill and agoraphobic to go out as they have released me on a Friday and I have to ask the au pair to go and buy Lilla a diamond bracelet and earrings and a bottle of the finest champagne. I order from the best Italian restaurant the most expensive dishes for home delivery. I know the chef and he says *he will make them himself for my beautiful lady*.

Or my beautiful demon. I don't know what she is.

Lilla loves the bracelet and earrings but the champagne is wasted on both of us. Neither of us really wants to drink it but I thought it might help break down the distance between us. She feels ill after 2 flutes of it and it gives her a headache and I thought it would make her happy even though I don't believe she should drink when she is depressed and pregnant, but I want to do anything to make her feel good tonight. It mixes badly with my meds and I fall off my chair after a couple of flutes and she has to leave our dinner half eaten and help me to bed as my head is spinning. She leaves the champagne on the table and Natalija drinks a glass and as Lilla is putting me to bed, Natalija runs in and throws her plush dinosaurs in the air and leaps on the bed, smacking the bedside lamp to the floor. She is laughing and falling over.

"She's drunk, Lilla. Natalija, did you drink the adult drink?"

"Just one, just one," laughs Natalija falling on her back.

"It's my fault. I should have put the champagne in the fridge. I'm sorry, István," Lilla says. "Children normally hate the taste of alcohol, I didn't think. I'm really sorry."

Natalija lies on her back laughing like crazy and I am too sleepy to be angry.

I am out cold.

Lilla is busy in work and it is like she has never been away. She tries her best at home, she tries to cook for me but we know she has destroyed all my trust. We talk about shallow and pointless topics, we are existing on this dull path, avoiding the passion and the love and hate. It is boring but it is keeping me sane for the moment. I know Lilla will most likely explode again, like the volcanoes in the Timanfaya national park, that all her passion and anger is still enough to burn me down to the bone.

But I am in way too deep to drag myself out of the crater.

The age gap has made my usual jealousy burn with a murderous intensity, there is no rationality. Any young man she talks to in work is a threat even though she is pregnant. Any of them. I do not consider she may be lonely, she may just be friendly, she may just be nice. I assume she is fucking or wanting to fuck all of them because I know men and they are always transfixed by Lilla so I cannot believe she would be loyal.

CARMEN

It is July and I think I truly hate Lilla. She has had her c-section at the hospital and told me she didn't want me there. "Why would I want you there?" she said angrily. "I don't need you to hold my goddamn hand."

I don't say how much this hurts me for so many reasons. I go to visit her the day after her surgery and the hospital staff are cool with me. When I took Lilla there I gave them all big tips so why are they so hostile now? What poison has my Lilla been telling them? One nurse makes her feelings clear. "She's been waiting for you. She's just a young girl. She was alone and crying in the operating theatre. Why weren't you here? She told me her husband was a cruel older man and she's right."

She snatches the roses I have brought for Lilla out of my hands and I try to explain Lilla didn't want me here, she told me no way was I to be there but the nurse has gone off ahead of me to Lilla with the flowers.

"He's finally here, sweetheart," she says kindly to Lilla as she puts the flowers in water. Then the nurse glares at me and walks off. I give her another roll of money as she leaves the room and she just grabs it from my hands, stuffs it in her pocket and stalks out without another word.

Lilla looks at me and looks through me. She looks so pale and delicate I feel such tenderness for her. I stroke her hair from her face and kiss her and she moves her face away. I ask her how she is.

"I'm sorry you didn't want me there, Lilla. The nurse told me you were crying in the operating theatre. I should have been there to hold your hand," I say as I sit next to her.

"Why do you fucking think I wanted you there to

enjoy me being sliced open?" She snaps at me and turns to face the window. "Sadist," she mutters.

Does she really think I only wanted to be there to watch her being hurt? She really hates me.

I turn my attention to Levente in his crib. "Can I hold him, Lilla?" I ask picking him up gently.

"Do what the Hell you want," she says. "You do anyway. He's yours now. I do not want him."

I am sad she is behaving like this. I wanted to be there for her but she told me no way. I wasn't going to force her to have me there. I am not angry with her as I know she must be in pain with her stomach wound. I ask her *is she hurting, does she need more pain relief?*

No, I can deal with it. The nurses are nice, she says.

Lilla, I say. *I wish you would just tell me what I can do. If there is anything to make whatever it is you are going through easier, I will do it. You know that when you come home, you will have help 12 hours a day. Kata will be there all the time to help and the cleaner will do everything. You don't need to worry.*

She says nothing. I put down Levente. I know she hasn't even looked at him. He is delicate with black curly hair and she hates him because she knows he will look like me.

"I got you something," I tell her and I hand her a wrapped box with a silver and ruby necklace she admired when we were out one day. She opens the box and picks out the necklace, looks at it without a smile and puts it back in the box and next to her on the bedside cabinet.

"Don't you like it?" I ask. "You saw it that time we were out for dinner and I thought you loved it. Don't you want me to put it on you?"

She sighs and hands me the box and I gently fasten the necklace around her. She is in pain trying to sit up more.

Let me help you, baby, I say as I reach forward.

Don't touch me. I don't want you. All you ever want to do is fuck, she snarls at me. *You're an animal and I hate you.*

"That necklace is as beautiful as you are," I say. I ignore her nasty comments but they cut me open. I love her and I just want to care for her right now. I smile at her. Even angry she is so beautiful. She stares at me coldly, her eyes full of hatred.

She doesn't even say thank you. The only question she asks is, "When are you taking me home? I've had it with the hospital. I'm not sick, I don't need to be here."

"You do, baby. You just had a major stomach operation. I can't take you today, Lilla. They need to make sure your stomach is healing."

"Fine, tomorrow then. You can pick me up tomorrow," she says turning away from me.

"It might be too early," I tell her.

"Fucking tomorrow, okay?" she says turning around to face me. She looks at me with such hatred it breaks my heart.

I say *I will talk to the staff.*

I leave the room and say that I hope she feels better tomorrow and I realise I am crying. Because she is so cold. Because she obviously hates me, hates Levente and even though she is in pain she wants to get out so she can get on with her normal life.

I have to pick her up with Levente. She is leaving early against hospital advice with her stomach stapled up and trying to pretend she is not in pain and she doesn't want to touch this lovely boy. I know she can't lift him with her freshly stitched wound but she doesn't even want him near her. I am trying to be patient and I knew she would be like this so I have reasoned she might not connect with him for a while. I have to be patient. She is in pain with her operation and I have to treat her like crystal.

Natalija has picked up the same indifference towards her new brother, probably as a result of Lilla.

I am grateful in a way because Natalija could have felt like she was being replaced. As soon as Lilla arrived back from the hospital Natalija is waiting like an adoring puppy and Lilla smiles and takes her hand and goes to her room to play. Levente seems like he is not flesh and blood to her. Natalija just has one curious look at Levente and asks me is he a doll? Then she rushes off before the answer. I despise Lilla for her hatred of Levente but at least Natalija has her love and attention.

Kata takes our son from me without judgement of Lilla and says *sometimes this happens, the way Lilla is. People react differently and Lilla could take time.*

She hates me, I say. *She really hates me.*

"Give her time, István," she says squeezing my hand. "She is so young, she hides a lot. It doesn't mean she hates him or you. She is in pain and her emotions will be all over the place. I am here to help her all day every day for as long as it takes."

But I know she does hate me. Very much. I offer to help her change the dressing on her stomach and she tells me to go to Hell. She is in the bathroom struggling to do it herself and throws the roll of bandages at me when I try to go in. "Get the Hell out, I don't want you. I never did!" she screams.

Lilla is no doubt suffering from an angry depression herself but Kiára was never like this. I try my best to help her. The au pair and cleaner do everything. She refuses to even look at Levente. I try everything to make her happy but she still hates me. I am gentle, I tell her I love her and I don't make her take care of Levente. I am doing everything at night when the au pair isn't here. I have to see to him as she just lies in bed and covers her head with the pillow if he cries. She would just leave him to cry if I didn't get up to see to him.

I am so angry with her one night as she is sitting up in bed when I had to get up and see to him. She laughs at me in a nasty way which makes me mad as she could have got up herself if she is awake, she just didn't want to touch her lovely little boy. This makes me lose my control and I get back into bed and kiss her hard and pull her hair and she bites my shoulder and scratches me telling me *she hates me, she hates me so much she feels her heart will explode.*

Good, I whisper in her ear. *Good, because I really fucking hate you too. And I mean hate, Lilla. I never hated anyone as much in my life.* And the old passion stirs and I forget myself as her claws dig deeper into my back tearing into my flesh.

Then she is crying so much I think she is laughing. "Lilla," I say. "Lilla, baby. Did I hurt you? Did I hurt your stomach?"

She shakes her head and rolls onto her side and cries so much into the pillow it is breaking my heart to hear her. I try to hold her telling her *I didn't mean what I said, I was tired. I hate her sometimes, but she hates me too but you have to love to hate, darling. Please believe me.*

God we are so fucked up. I am holding her telling her how much I love her and she is crying most of the night. She gives in and lets me check her stomach wound but it seems like it is healing fast. She lets me hold her as I promise we are going to make sure she is better soon.

Actually, I am lying. I have no idea how I can make it better. I have no idea how to help this girl who is my wife. I am lost.

I am working long hours and I am tired and irritable as I have had a month of broken sleep due to getting up to see to Levente. It has only been a few times in the night but it is enough to mess up my sleep cycle. As I am rising into my up-state I am feeling a strange sort of manic and I am in an agitated mixed episode. I am frenzied with a low and angry mood but combined with the energy of mania; a lethal combination. I can only take so much. I am so angry I have a thought which goes round and round in my head of driving my car at 200 kmph and smashing into a motorway bridge and leaving everyone.

One Friday night after I got home late after a stressful day, cooked this ungrateful girl dinner and she toys with it sullenly not wanting to talk to me, I grab the casserole dish and hurl it across the kitchen. I am glad Natalija is not here but at a friend's house this weekend as I would hate her to see this although I think I would have thrown the dish anyway, given the black mood I am in.

"Enough!" I scream. "I have had enough, Lilla!"

She sits up in fear as the dish shatters against the wall and I am shouting at her *I am King István and she is my wife. I am not some doormat husband. You were home first. Why the fuck didn't you cook? Because you are fucking useless, that's why. And I am going out tonight. Sit here and sulk alone. You are so boring! You are the most boring woman I could ever be with*, I say. *I should never have married you. In fact I wish I never met you! I should be with someone else, not you!*

I am cruel but I am mad tonight.

I go and get my coat and she tries to take my arm. I wrench away from her.

"Get out of my way, Lilla. Don't make me hurt you," I say. "God, I can't wait for you to make up your mind what or who you want and then you can just go as whatever I do is not good enough. I have really had enough of you."

Spoilt little bitch.

She sees my dark, angry expression and moves to let me pass.

"I don't want you to go, please don't leave tonight, István. Don't leave me alone," she says to my back as I walk down the apartment steps.

"You are not alone. You can take care of your son, Lilla," I call back.

Why is it anger and hurting her is the only way to get through to this girl?

I actually really hate her so much. If she was sad, depressed and crying I could deal with any amount of it and I would understand. But it is this careless indifference, her ingratitude, her hatred of me and Levente that really makes me resent her.

I don't care if she leaves me now. I have my son. I don't need her.

Fuck her. I give her everything, I buy everything, I am trying to be as gentle and nice as I can and I get nowhere. What did I ever see in her apart from the ghost of my dead love? I am so sick of her. The shrink was so right; I will not find Kiára in this girl.

I decide I am going to go to a bar, not a travellers' bar but a classy bar and I am going to pick up a woman and get well and truly laid without guilt then go home around midnight. I find the sultriest brunette and work my magic and the next morning when I wake up somewhere in the XIII district in this woman's bed it is 9 in the morning. I switch on my phone. 37 missed calls all from the house phone and from Lilla's cell phone and endless texts. I didn't mean to fall asleep and stay all night but a glass of wine with meds knocked me out as I have been so tired with my broken sleep pattern this month. The woman who I think is called Zsofi asks *do I have to go?* She is still drunk and half asleep.

"Sorry, baby. I do have to go but I have your number."

Fragments

But I won't be calling it. She is just a one nighter. It was okay, it stopped me thinking but I hate what I have become. The idea of cheating on Kiára would never have entered my head, ever. No matter how angry she was, how volcanic our arguments.

I let myself out and take a taxi. The sun is up and it is going to be another airless, boiling hot day. I look out across the Duna River as the taxi crosses the bridge and I see the Szabadság Híd in the distance where Kiára jumped from in desperation ironically as she thought I was cheating on her when she had post-natal depression. I cover my eyes and look away. It is too much, even now. Especially what I have just done. I have done exactly what Kiára feared I was doing. And I never meant to stay more than a few hours. I have stayed out all night and that is unforgiveable. Cheating on Lilla is unforgiveable, no matter how horrible she is right now.

I close my eyes when we cross the river as I always do or stare directly ahead when I am driving.

Last night's payback cheating has left me feeling ill. How could I have left Lilla alone? I was only going to go out for a few hours to get her in a better mood and stupidly, I fell asleep and stayed out all night. And I cheated, God I am evil. I cheated on her.

She was acting moody and cold but the poor girl only had Levente a month ago. Who knows what depression she is dealing with? Her indifference and sullen behaviour is just the way her depression manifests itself.

A voice in my head says, 'If she kills herself it will be your fault'.

'Please,' I beg the voice. 'Please let her be okay. I will never forgive myself.'

I open my front door and Lilla is in the living room curled up with a blanket and a box of tissues.

"Where's Natalija?" I ask.

"Ice skating probably, she is at her friend's house this weekend. Don't you remember?" asks Lilla. She gets up and says, "Where were you? Where the Hell were you, István? You were out all night. I called and called you. I was sick with worry." She looks wild-haired, make-up streaked with tears but so beautiful. Always so beautiful and I want to say I am sorry but I don't.

"Not nice, baby, is it? Imagine that feeling every day for a month like I had with you in March. Oh, but you wouldn't know I called as your phone was here," I say sarcastically.

I see her mascara all over her face; she hasn't slept and I feel sorry and guilty. She steps closer to me.

"Fucking perfume all over you, all over your neck and hair!" she screams inhaling it. She grabs hold of my hair and forces me to look at her. I look at her and my eyes are full of contempt.

"You were fucking someone weren't you? You went out all night and fucked someone!" she is hysterical and slaps my face. I turn away. It doesn't hurt, she is not strong enough. I am angry but I am not going to hit her. Ever. She slaps me again screaming, "I hate you! I fucking hate you!"

I deserve her hatred. I hate me too.

She leaps at me trying to scratch me calling me a bastard, calling me every name she can, spitting them out in her rage. I hold her arms still and pull her into me. "Shhh, Lilla. It's okay. I am here now. Stop struggling, you'll hurt yourself. Your stomach hasn't healed yet."

"You made me feel I was going crazy, you cheated on me. I had your son a month ago and you are already out fucking. You spent the whole night out and fucked someone," she is crying so hard she can hardly stand.

"Yes, I am not going to lie but I did it because you

are not nice to me, Lilla and other people are. You fight me and say you hate me....." I say softly into her hair. I hold her up to stop her collapsing in a heap on the floor. I kiss her lovely neck as I am holding her so tight she can't move.

"I do fucking hate you! I hate you! And I never wanted your bastard kid." She has lost it and she is crying and crying and I hold her and tell her *I am sorry. I did it to hurt her. I am the bastard and I am sorry I pressurised her for too much too soon.* I sit her down on the sofa and she cries for an hour and she lets me hold her and stroke her hair because what else can we do? We could fight some more, hate each other some more and carry on living in misery.

"You're breaking my heart," she says into my chest and I hold her tighter.

And you are breaking mine, my ice princess.

I despise myself for cheating and hurting her but it shocks her at least for the moment and she stops her terrible behaviour. I just don't know why I have to do this to get her to be nice or why we have to hurt each other so much. I would never have even thought of cheating on Kiára. I know this relationship is sick, twisted and horribly damaged. I know the foundations are so fragile and I know why she is here in the first place; because of her looks, because it is the closest I can get to Kiára and probably ever can.

She returns to work for the last few days before the national holiday. I don't want her to, but if she needs to, I am not going to stop her. She is broken by me and sad and everyone is asking about the baby but she just shrugs and says he is fine.

She doesn't want to talk to them and she is being sweet and obedient towards me at home but she still won't see to Levente apart from the night I cheated on her. He was fed and changed then but she won't do it now. Even Natalija has crept into his room curious and said, "He's sweet, mama. Don't you like him? He has black curly hair like me."

Lilla has said *boys and men are not for her; they are cruel, not like her princess Natalija.*

"And he is all István, none of him is mine," she says.

"Really?" Natalija says. "Am I all István too?"

"No, sweet girl. You look like him but you have your mama's and István's blood in you."

"Oh," Natalija says confused.

What the Hell is wrong with Lilla? Is she actually believing that herself because it sounds like it.

I just don't know how to talk to her about it. She needs a goddamn shrink to tell her that Levente is her flesh and blood too. And Natalija is going to grow up thinking all men are sadists. Lilla probably tells her even more when I am not listening.

I wonder if she has psychotic depression.

And later in August I am there on the phone as I am in America for two weeks for a conference. I am talking to her every day. I am sorry for her. She is 19 and vulnerable and I just left her while the au pair is looking after our son who is only a month old and Lilla is too depressed to get out of bed since the dental surgery is closed for 10 days for the holidays. So I call her at the same time every day and she is in bed. I speak to Natalija and tell Lilla that I love her, I love her more than anything. And I think I do.

I have to have a different au pair for the nights as I cannot guarantee Lilla will get out of bed.

This is very sad. I just explain to the temporary help that my wife is ill with depression and I need her to be there at night to keep watch on her too.

I am also terrified as I went to a conference in America soon after Kiára had Natalija and she attempted suicide when I was away. I had called her every day in America but it still did not keep her safe.

But I cheat on Lilla again in America. Maybe because she pushed me too far. I am still hurting for her runaway act in April, which devastated me so I cheat with one woman I find attractive, but not much more and she knows I am married and it is never going anywhere. It is cold, metallic hotel room sex. Can't remember your name and don't really care who you are and where you are from, only we both want to have sex. And as I lie in bed with this woman, I realise that Lilla has changed me. I have become cruel, controlling, sadistic, lying and a cheat. I always was hard and sadistic and Kiára and I both hurt each other but after her death, I was cut to pieces and completely broken. Then I found Lilla and gave her too much, spoilt her with material goods, possessed her free spirit and we ended up destroying each other. I have got much sicker since I married Lilla and the sweet girl I found has cut me to pieces so I hurt her, she hurts me and it never ends.

On the plane back to Hungary I see myself in the glass of my window seat and see a handsome but cruel man, someone who hurts people because he can. I think I would never ever have cheated on Kiára in a million years, however difficult and angry she became. Because I loved her like nothing else in the world and now here I am cheating again and not even because I want to. Not even because I have found someone else. Just because I can. And I despise myself for it.

Lilla is still sweet. She is waiting in the apartment with flowers for me and Natalija rushes to the door happy I am back. Lilla says *she missed me so much*. This time she would never know I cheated and I would not tell her; I will even lie if she does ask. I don't want to hurt her anymore. But the poor girl cries every night. I know this time I haven't hurt her,

I am treating her like crystal and I hold her and ask her *what is wrong; is her stomach wound still hurting?* She won't speak so I just hold her and tell her she can talk to me when she needs to.

And I have cheated three times. The only cheating she might have done is in my head. I have no proof she cheated when her friend came over for coffee, I could have been paranoid. But I know I have cheated with three different women. I am a bastard.

'But she left you, she left you and gave you a breakdown,' the voice in my head says. 'And never even called you, not once in 3 weeks.'

I look at the photo of Kiára as Lilla sleeps and I long for her. Lilla looks exactly like this photo but she is a child, I married a child. I made one Hell of a mistake, I think as I stroke her hair and look at her calm face with those long black eyelashes. She looks so young, so fragile. A young messed up version of my dead love. 'I'm so sorry Lilla. I messed up your life. I wish I could put it right again.'

I wish we could start again and go back to that January when I met you and was transfixed and you were sweet and lovely. I wish. Would I have done everything differently? Would I have treated you more gently? Would I have taken my time and not tried to control and rush everything which is maybe why you ran away in March? I think I made you run away, by my controlling behaviour.

Goddamn her. Her sweetness does not last. It never does. What makes her change? I have no idea.

It is literally as though a switch snaps out this sweet, gentle Lilla into a raging demon. She seems cold and indifferent and she starts going out on weekends in late September with a stomach wound that has just healed, getting smashed and ending up staggering back into the apartment at 4 or 5 in the morning. I find her passed out on the sofa, the floor of the bathroom, even the stairwell one morning. I hate her like this but I am past arguing and controlling her. She has a heart of ice that girl. She cares very little about anyone, especially Levente although she is still loving towards Natalija. She hurts me emotionally and I hurt her physically and the mess of our marriage is lying scattered on the floor.

I ask Lilla *how are you so heartless? How can you go out drinking just leaving us?*

She says *she is making up for lost time, she couldn't face alcohol much after feeling depressed and before she had Levente and now she wants to enjoy herself.*

Enjoy herself. So she does not enjoy our beautiful home, our love, our lovely little girl and her son? She just wants to go out and get wrecked and maybe fuck some young men. I have tried to give her everything, but she has smashed the amber palace to pieces, my cold ice queen and now the jagged splinters of amber are scattered on the ground. It hurts to walk on them.

I am crazy with worry when she is out so drunk and out of control; I am not sleeping until I hear her crash in at some ungodly hour. The au pair is having to be here all hours of the day because I cannot make Lilla love him. She won't even give him his bottle when I hold it out for her.

"I don't want to touch him," she says angrily. "You give him his bottle, you wanted him. He can starve to death for all I care."

I want to shake her for that, I want to scream at her but I just let it go. Heartless girl. She would leave him to starve, the demon she is.

People ask me why Lilla is not taking more time off and I just say *she wants to work, leave us alone. She likes her work.* I do not tell them she hates me and she hates our son. I do not tell them a damn thing about us.

I know everyone thinks we are both strange. They

are right.

I try locking her in the apartment one weekend and hiding the keys as I am tired of her wild behaviour. I am sick of her going out with God knows who. She goes mad that night and tries to climb out of the window and the cold autumn wind is rushing in and she is half-in and half-out of the second floor and she slips in her heels, screaming.

I drag her back in by her coat and say, "Lilla, stop this right now. Either stop this or leave me. I can't take it any longer. You are affecting my work. I am exhausted. And you don't fucking eat, what is wrong with you?"

We collapse on the floor and I close the window. She lies on the floor breathless, her lovely face dark with anger, hating me. Her silver dress glitters and she is wearing the silver shoes I bought her when we first met. *What went wrong Lilla? Where is that lovely girl I first met? Did I turn you into this?*

Be careful what you wish for.

Then her dark expression turns into sorrow and she cries and cries and cries. Her body is still flooded with hormones she doesn't understand and she needs help. She says her stomach is hurting her. She fell over drunk last weekend and thinks she tore something. We are making each other sicker. The cleaner is doing everything in the house as Lilla won't do a thing. I just hope she can get through this. I still have to get up in the night if Levente needs seeing to. I don't mind now. I am not sleeping too well and he sleeps most of the night anyway.

Lilla's mother has not called. She was true to her word when she said she didn't want to see her grandchild and I think *what an unfeeling horrible bitch to not even mellow when she has this lovely little boy and doesn't even call to see if Lilla is coping.*

It explains a lot of Lilla's reckless behaviour. The fact her mother doesn't even care enough to send flowers or call her, let alone see her. Her only child and she doesn't give a damn and it isn't just because she married me. There is a lot more to it than that.

I carry Lilla to the bedroom and she doesn't protest; she is clinging to my neck. She is hysterical and I am afraid Kiára's spirit is possessing Lilla, turning her into a depressed and angry girl. I look at her sleeping later and this is too much for me. I will be the one running away soon.

I cannot understand this girl. I cannot understand how she has changed. Each time I decide I can't carry on with this insane existence, I wake up next to her and I know I would last a day without her and I would be lost.

After that my stupid heart would be crying for her again and I can't have poor Natalija hurt again if Lilla is not here.

I also cannot understand her indifference towards her lovely son who is so undemanding; he rarely cries and she does not want to go near him. Yet she still couldn't face going for a termination despite her protests of not wanting him. She still has plenty of time for Natalija. My shrink has told me she is too young. I have pushed her into too much and taken her freedom and her unresolved post-traumatic stress disorder from seeing her beloved father take his own life is not helping. Her mother is obviously cold and uncaring as well.

Lilla needs help and she needs medication. She is sick.

She refuses to see a shrink but she has told me on the rare occasions she is not hating me, some things about the loss she felt with her father's violent death and how she started shutting everyone out just as I did when I lost my parents when I was at university.

"I just want to feel something, anything. I just can't seem to feel, I don't feel real."

I put my arms around her. *Lilla, I would do anything to help if only I knew what to do.*

"Lilla, I heard what you said to Natalija about Levente being only me, nothing of you. I hope you know that isn't true, don't you?"

She says *she doesn't know. He doesn't feel real. He doesn't feel like anything to do with her at all.* She gave him a bottle the night I stayed out all night but says she felt nothing for him and still doesn't.

"Lilla, you need help. Please see a doctor, for me," I tell her.

I wonder if she can truly love anything or anyone. I wonder why she seems calmer and almost loving when I am ill and cannot be nice to me when I am well.

The shrink has told me *not to push her anymore. She might leave for good. I should not have pressurised her into so much so soon and dragged her out of university due to my violent jealousy. She is only 19 years old, the shrink tells me. Maybe she needs you to show her off. Maybe she wants you to show how proud you are to be with her. Try to take her out and show her to the world.*

He again, is not telling me I am a bad man. He genuinely wants to help us. He saw the shrapnel of my personality all over the apartment and then the hospital ward after I had a complete breakdown due to Lilla at the end of May. He knows he cannot offer a serious long term solution but if anything will help, he will suggest it. I have confided in him I will kill myself or her if she runs away again. I thought I could manage without her, but the truth is more complex. I am addicted to her; I am obsessed with Lilla and as horrible and icy as she has become, I cannot live without her.

Fragments

I decide to take Lilla out for the evening to the most romantic restaurant I can find. She has hardly eaten since having Levente and I am worried about her health. I hope the delicious food will tempt her. I have bought her a dress and shoes in Gucci and silk underwear. I dress her and hope I can make her smile. She lets me put on her underwear and I look at her perfect body but she says as she looks in the mirror,

"Damn, I need to lose a kilo or two round my middle and damn Levente, look at this ugly scar."

"No, sweetheart, you are perfect. You don't have to be size zero. You are so beautiful. And the scar is a reminder of your lovely son," I tell her smiling at her.

She looks at me like I am stupid. 'You stupid man,' is in her smouldering eyes. 'You understand nothing'.

"Well I am so glad I've got the IUD now because I am not having any more pill-related accidents, there will be no more heirs to the throne, King István. I did my bit. You can find your third wife for the next," she laughs nastily. "You sure get through the women in this country."

I don't say anything. I don't say there won't be a third wife because you will be here, Lilla until I die. I want you with me forever whatever poison you spit at me now.

"And you just picked me up on the street. What kind of man does that?" she looks down at me with contempt as I open the box with new shoes for her.

"Because you were the most beautiful girl I had ever seen. I hadn't dated anyone since...."

"Yeah, I know. You picked me up because I look like her," she says angrily.

What does she think of me if that is how she sees me? I am not arguing with her tonight.

I fasten her into her dress, red with gold shoes and tell her she is beautiful. She says nothing, not even a smile.

She drinks too much in the restaurant but at least she laughs, at least she shows some interest in eating. It is a change from her glaring at me or sticking her claws into my back in bed. My back is raw with scratches like I have a cat mauling it every night. I forgot in the locker room in work one morning and one of the dentists said, "My God, István. You've got a wild one there. She looks so sweet but she's a tiger" and laughed. I am more careful now, wearing a t-shirt under my dental whites as I get changed.

Lilla says *I try to make love to her and she makes hate to me. I am a good fuck, the best and laughs*. This leads to huge arguments as the comment suggests she has slept with other lovers. She denies it and says *it is not true. I am just a good fuck that's all.*

She is abrupt with me in work these days as well and people ask *is something wrong?*

"Nothing is wrong, she is just trying to cope and it is difficult for her. She is young and she has a full-time job and her stepdaughter to care for and she is still brittle after having our son, why can't everyone leave us alone?" I shout at another concerned person. I am angry.

I just tell them *she likes her job, it is important that she works.*

I would be afraid if she was left at home in case she is hiding her depression, as Kiára did. I suspect she is and her depression is coming out in anger and indifference. I know I can make sure she is okay when she is in work and she can still smile for the customers, she is able to hold it together or act, whatever she is doing in this web of deceit.

Tonight I want her to see how much she means to me despite her rages and moods.

"Lilla," I take her hand at the restaurant table as

she laughs at something. "Lilla if I did things I shouldn't, and I know I did, I wish you would forgive me. I wish you would talk to me. The only time we connect is in bed and I am your husband. I made you give up a lot. I made you give up your freedom, university, I was demanding you give me a child and maybe this is the main problem. I know you never wanted him. I know you think I hate you for not caring about him, but I am trying to understand and it must have been so hard for you and maybe you will love him in your own time. And I am sick with bipolar and I know it must be so difficult for you. After what you went through with your father."

She looks down. She pokes at the remains of our shared tiramisu with her fork.

"Lilla please, I am trying to help. You are so lovely when I am ill. You are so lovely with Natalija. I just don't know why you hate me so much. Why you hate that little boy so much who is yours not just mine."

Then she starts crying so loudly, probably the wine isn't helping, but the whole restaurant can hear and she covers her face and won't and can't stop. I hold her and she clings to me as I quickly pay the bill so I can get us out of here. Obviously, some of my words got through to her.

She cries all the way home in the taxi but at least she is holding on to me and not pushing me away screaming that she hates me. The au pair is surprised to see us in this state as I carry Lilla in, but she says *Natalija is asleep, Levente too, everything is fine.* She knows we are having problems.

I take Lilla to bed and through her tears she says, "Love me, show me you love me. Hurt me, do anything, bite me, thrash me, be rough, I need to feel something. Anything, I just need to feel."

"I can't hurt you tonight, Lilla. I can only love you. No matter how horrible you think you are towards me you will never drive me away, I will always be your István."

I hold her tightly as she sleeps with her head on my chest. I cannot get into her head. I know she is binge drinking to forget or suppress feelings. I won't stop her but I am so worried. I sweep the waves of her hair away.

I want to give up, I want to leave this girl who is impossible now.

But my heart will not let me. I bury my face in her lovely skin and hold her tight.

Lilla, my life. Please come back to me. Please go back to that sweet, lovely girl I met.

I find her out of bed in the morning and she is sitting in the nursery looking at Levente. She watches him sleep and there is such sadness in her eyes. Is she sad because she can't love him or because she does but can't show it? Either way it is the only time she has walked into the room and sat there like this.

"Don't you want to hold him, Lilla?" I ask gently. "He would want you to. Just for a few minutes."

She shakes her head.

"It's okay, just sit there if you feel better."

She reaches a tentative hand through the bars of the crib as if she is going to stroke him, then pulls it away again and wraps her arms under her knees.

I have booked her in with expensive psychologists and psychiatrists all over Buda but she never attends. I cannot force her because even if I dragged her there she could sit in frozen silence for hours and not speak a word. My ice princess.

The one appointment she did attend she hardly spoke and the shrink told me *she wasn't ready so there was no point booking her in again. Bring her back when she will talk,* he said.

I take my ice princess to the opera house. Carmen is on. How fitting; I do not realise that later it will be even more relevant. She doesn't seem happy; she agrees to go and says *she doesn't think she will like it.*

"How do you know, you never go to opera? Kiára loved opera."

"Kiára, Kiára, Kiára. I am not her," says Lilla angrily in the bedroom. She is in a red dress

You are the image of her. God, I wish you had her personality.

Beautiful, with her hair put up into diamond pins and her fur. I am so proud to show her off. Everyone looks at her in the opera house.

One man says, "Carmen; a wonderful Carmen that girl."

Lilla is not saying much but I can see she is transfixed by the performance and at the end she cries and says, "How beautiful, how sad."

She holds onto me and the tears are falling down her face. We get in the taxi and the avenue looks so beautiful at night with the opera house lit up. "I can't stop crying," she says. It has reached into her heart and touched her deeply. She leans against me in the taxi, holding me tight.

"You're being very nice, my Lilla," I say.

"If I betrayed you would you stab me to death too?" she asks looking at me.

"Lilla I could never do that to anyone especially you."

"But you hate me sometimes, don't you?"

"Yes, at times I do," I tell her. "But you hate me too."

"If I betray you, please will you kill me," she says suddenly after a few minutes' silence.

The bridges over the river are lit up and the glowing gold castle is lovely in the blackness and this dark moment.

"Lilla, what are you saying. I would never kill you. Why are you talking like this?"

She holds my arm tighter. She says no more and I wrap my arm round her shoulders as we go back into the apartment. Tonight she is different, a soft thoughtful Lilla. But dark. I am starting to wonder if she has a personality disorder.

DESTRUCTION

Lilla is talking to Krisztina in the living room and doesn't hear me open the front door quietly. It is a Saturday in December and I had to go into work to perform emergency surgery. Lilla was supposed to care for Levente while Kata took Natalija for her ice-skating training but more than likely poor Kata had to take Levente with her.

Lilla is talking loudly so I hear everything. I look through the chink in the door and see her lovely and angelic in cream lace, more beautiful and more like Kiára than when I first met her.

But she is a demon underneath all her beauty and the anger is evident in her voice.

"István. He seduced me when I had never even been with a man and he wanted me to marry him when I was just turned 18." She spits out the words like poison as she says this.

"I was in love with him and I thought he was the most handsome man in the world and then on our wedding night he virtually raped me. He is sex-addicted. He forced me to have his so called 'heir to the throne' when I was only 19 and should have been at university. He is so obsessed with carrying on his bloodline. What about girls, are they not enough? Wasn't Natalija enough? Natalija is not my flesh and blood but I love her as though she is. She is a girl. I cannot love a boy, especially one in the image of my husband."

This shocks people when she admits it so coldly; they do not know what to say to that. There is no love in her ice cold heart.

I feel like my soul is sliding away. 'The image of my husband'. Those words stab with a fierce intensity and I slowly open the door and walk into the room and Lilla turns round and sees me.

"István, I didn't hear you come back," she says without a hint of regret. She must know I heard what she said. I turn away, unable to speak.

Krisztina, embarrassed by Lilla's comments says she has to leave now.

"Have a nice Christmas, Doktor Úr," she says politely as she leaves. She is also lost for words at Lilla's apparent hatred of me. She had probably called round to see Levente, although he is not here.

The au pair is doing everything even on a weekend. This also makes me mad. The least Lilla could have done was to spend a few hours with her son while Kata went to the ice rink with Natalija. I would pay for Lilla to have driving lessons so she could take Natalija but given her rages, I do not want Lilla behind the wheel of my car especially with my daughter in it.

When Lilla shuts the door behind Krisztina, I grab hold of her by her shoulders. "Don't you ever, ever show me up like that again. Do you fucking hear me?"

She tells me *to stop it, I am hurting her.*

"I am your husband and you never disrespect me like that or you can fuck off back to your dark XIV district. Everything, Lilla. I have tried to give you everything and you throw it all back at me."

I don't realise I am shaking her and she cries out, "Stop it, you scare me when you are like this."

"You told your friend I raped you on your wedding night. How could you? She'll think I am a monster?" I am so mad at her for telling people about our sex life.

"Well you were a bit goddamn rough, István. I was just a girl." She looks at me burning with passion and hate. But mainly hate.

"I didn't rape you, did I baby? Please tell me I didn't." I hold her face and look into those beautiful eyes. She looks at me and then grabs my hair and violently kisses me biting my lip.

"Fuck, Lilla. That hurt." There is blood on my lips.

"Well you are such a sex-crazed lunatic. Are you going to want Natalija when she's older?"

She looks at me smouldering with rage. She is a feral cat with her biting and scratching.

I grab her hair and push her into the wall. "Don't you ever, ever say that. Natalija is my little girl and I would sooner die than touch her. You are sick, you bitch." I pull her hair harder and bite her throat and the pain makes her cry out and she says, "You are a bastard, a cruel monster. I hate you and I wish I never met you!"

We are wild animals fighting and hurting and being hurt. I pull up her skirt and she drags her claws down my back so hard my skin is under her nails and sinks her fangs into my shoulder.

I think as I shower afterwards she is turning into the kind of lover I want.

It is also the one place I go to cry alone when Lilla hurts me. Not physically but emotionally. She hates me no matter what I do. And the comment about Natalija is burning. Even if she was being nasty, the way she said that I would want my own daughter for sex is sick. Kiára once said something like that in an argument and it makes me ill. My pure little Natalija. If Natalija climbed into my bed in silk underwear at age 15, I would be horrified. I would never touch her, whatever she did. She will always be my little girl.

The soap is in my eyes when Lilla is standing there in front of the shower laughing at me. Fucking laughing because she can see me crying through the soap and the running water. I would never laugh at her crying, no matter how cruel she has been or how difficult. When Lilla cries all I want to do is hold her. Yet here is this angel turned demon with a sarcastic smile on her face enjoying my pain. I lean out of the shower and drag her in and we are fighting each other again, unrestrained and angry. Until I slip on the soap and we fall out still clutching each other and she smacks her head on the bathroom sink with a horrible crack.

She flops to the ground and is silent and still and her eyes are closed like a china doll with those long black eyelashes. There is blood from her head on the white towel mat. My heart is racing. I can't breathe. I have killed her. Her words *'would you kill me if I betrayed you?'* have come true.

"Lilla, oh God, Lilla," I say and I am checking her pulse and breathing and she is not dead.

Lilla please wake up. I wrap myself in my gown and run out for my phone and I dial 104 as Lilla groans "My fucking head. What did I do?"

"Lilla, baby. Your head is bleeding. We should get you to hospital," I am frantic I have hurt her badly as she took the full weight of me falling.

She sees the blood on the rug. "Fuck, what happened?" She sits up and holds her head. "I feel dizzy."

I take a towel and hold it to stop the bleeding. "We need to go to hospital, baby."

"No, I am okay. You're an animal, István. Were you trying to do it again?" then she laughs.

"It's not funny, Lilla. I thought you were dead," I say. "We were fighting in the shower and I slipped on the soap and then we fell."

She laughs like crazy at this.

"Lilla it is not funny," I tell her. "And I think you need to see a doctor."

She refuses to go to hospital but I tell her any changes we are going. I take off her wet clothes and wrap her in her dressing gown and lift her up and carry her to bed and tell her *she is not to sleep, she is to sit here and talk and tell me why she hates me so much.*

"Did you do this?" she says as I am holding an ice pack wrapped in a towel to her head.

"No but I slipped on the soap when we were fighting in the shower. You were laughing because I was crying so I dragged you in there with me. I was angry," I tell her.

"I did? We did?" she can't remember. She is laughing again. But it is hysterical laughter which turns into tears and I don't know if her head injury has made her emotional but I think she definitely has a personality disorder.

She tells me she keeps fucking it up between us, she cries and laughs and I worry about her head wound and the au pair returns from the ice rink with Natalija and Levente and asks *why are we in bed at only 5 on a Saturday. Is Lilla okay? She is very pale.*

"I slipped in the shower, Kata and hit my head," she says. "I am okay now."

I get dressed as I need to see to the children.

When Kata leaves the room Lilla asks *did I try to kill her? Did I try and beat her head in on the sink?*

Her dark brown eyes question me seriously.

"Lilla, how can you say that? It was an accident. How can you think I would?"

Her eyes are depthless and expressionless. "I don't know why you wouldn't. You hate me, remember?"

I am about to tell her she hates me, I love her but Natalija runs in and wants to know *is Lilla sick?*

No, she fell and hurt herself, I tell her. *But why don't you bring your drawing books in here and talk to her while I make something to eat?*

Natalija agrees. She knows this is one of the few times she is allowed in here. I have always kept my bedroom as an adult zone and locked the door at night. I have been strict about this all along. There is no way children are getting in the way of my sex life. Ever.

Maybe because she hurt herself, Lilla is softer, emotional that night. I don't want her to sleep. I am afraid she will die in the night despite her protesting she feels fine, it just knocked her out; she is not sick or dizzy.

So I talk to her in the soft glow of the candles and she touches my skin gently and says she loves me so much her heart could explode but she keeps fucking it up. Something in her is telling her to destroy everything. "I want to ruin it all because I love you so much. I am sorry for what I said, about Natalija, about hating you, everything," she says and she looks so sad. "I am horrible."

"We can work it out," I promise her. "We will work it out. As long as it takes, Lilla. How could you even think I bashed your head on the bathroom sink deliberately? It was an accident; I was so scared you were dead. You were lying there still as a corpse and blood coming out of your head. You hit it so hard."

She laughs and strokes my hair and kisses my eyelids.

"I say terrible things. I just think sometimes you hate me so much you will end up killing me," she says. "I am not afraid of death."

"Lilla, my darling. Please don't say these things." But there is an element of truth in what she says and will be in the future. There are times I nearly kill both of us.

It is the last time I see the gentle Lilla for some time.

I don't sleep at all. I still worry she might die in the night after hitting her head. I watch over her in the glow of the nightlight and stroke her hair, keep checking her pulse and her breathing.

She is cheating on me. That winter with a new zest for life she goes around Budapest and takes lovers here there and everywhere to hurt me. I hope one day Levente breaks every woman's heart I am so bitter. I hope he hurts them all. No one has betrayed me with such treachery as Lilla.

I hope no one breaks Natalija's heart, my little girl. She is the real Kiára not this devil I am married to. But I hope Levente breaks everyone's heart. If he is anything like me, he will.

He will be a good-looking heartbreaker leaving devastated women all over the city.

I am glad.

Lilla has smashed my heart and soul to pieces and each time I fuck her I want to fuck her infidelity out of her. I want to make her want me so much she will never cheat again. I cannot cheat on her now and she wouldn't care anyway. She laughs when I am angry and digs her claws in my back and tells me *not to worry she had safe sex. I am her main lover.* I hurt her and she likes it. Her beautiful eyes look at me with contempt and hate and lust as she tells me *to go harder, hurt her, show her I am a man.* I bite her and choke her and she sighs in contentment. I shove her into the shower, against the sink taps and she is enjoying the pain. "Show me you're a man," she tells me each time. "Show me what you can do."

"Show me you're better than the others. For them I feel nothing."

"And what about me?" I ask her.

"I hate you, you know that."

"Don't you love me at all? You have to love to hate, Lilla."

"Yes, when I put my face into your neck and stroke your hair and see how handsome and kind you are. But then we both hate each other again and I am afraid if I really love you might leave me. If I let myself."

"I am not your father, Lilla. I know why you can't

love. I can't leave you even when you kill me with your infidelity, even when you have destroyed me and broken my heart. And no one ever broke my heart before, no woman." I mean that. *My Carmen.*

I taste salt on her face.

"Don't cry."

"I'm not fucking crying, István."

But I know she is.

"Why didn't you leave me when I cheated? I cheated so many times," she asks me.

"You know why. I love you, Lilla. Why didn't you leave me? You left me once. Why did you come back? And then I cheated on you, Lilla. I regret that so much."

She won't answer.

"If you hate me so much why are you still here? I know you love Natalija but is she the only reason to stay?"

"No," she sighs.

I reach over and pull her towards me and I feel her tears on my arms. I hold her tighter, squeezing her into me. My damaged Lilla. "Baby, I told you I would reshape the moon for you. I would do anything if I could help you. I know how much you were affected by your father's death. I wish you would just see someone to talk even if you can't talk to me. It won't go away, Lilla. You know it will only get worse and you must know you have changed so much from the Lilla I met on the street, that sweet girl."

She just reaches for the box of tissues and coils herself tighter around me, a python. I lick away her tears but she won't speak.

I wake up in the morning and she is wrapped around me so tightly I have to prise her hands off to get out of bed. She won't let go even in her sleep. In her sleep she whispers, "Tell István I love him, tell him because I can't. Tell him in case I die. Please tell him."

Why do you hurt the one you love so much, Lilla? Why can't you tell me you love me?

I kiss her lips but she doesn't stir. My angel demon.

I have to live with what is happening now. I can't make her do anything.

I am talking to the au pair and telling her one morning, "If anything happens to me, please make sure Natalija is taken care of. I have lots of money. It is all for her and Levente. My parents left me money years ago and it has built up in savings. I am rich. I have a will; it is all to go to them and not my wife. My lawyer has the will and his business card is in the top drawer next to my bed."

I changed the will when Lilla left me that time and I thought she would never return. I changed it so all my money and savings would go to any children I had.

"István, is there something wrong? Are you sick? Are you seriously ill? Do we need to get you help?" says Kata concerned. It is Christmas. I seem to be planning my death.

Over time I have confided in this woman, Kata. She knows about my severe bipolar illness.

But I tell her no, I am just worried, that is all. Just in case. I have no living family. I have a doctor friend, Zsolt from many years back in southern Hungary and he knows about the will. I have spoken to him on the phone many times when Lilla has not been around. He knows I have two separate wills. I changed my will from my first marriage when I married Lilla to split the money between her and Natalija and any other children we had, but the second one is for Natalija and Levente only which is cutting Lilla out entirely. I have told Zsolt I hope I will be using the first but I have to protect myself. Right now, if I died tomorrow, I would use the second will and Lilla would get nothing. I don't want this to happen but I can't leave my money to her when she is like this. Cheating and lying and hurting me. I am not going to have her spend my money on other men.

Lilla comes back that evening, her eyes bright with lust, hair dishevelled and I know she has cheated again. I want to kill her right now. I want to beat her until she is begging me for forgiveness. I have never wanted to beat a woman until I met Lilla. I am sexually violent and aggressive and controlling but hitting someone is beyond me. But I have fantasies about taking off my belt and thrashing Lilla across her back until she begs me to stop. It started when she ran away that time. I would never touch that lovely face. But I am too depressed to hurt her right now. I always know she has cheated as she is more affectionate and amorous. As though by sleeping with me she is atoning for her sins. What can I do with this woman who is so careless with my heart and has admitted she would not love her own son, because he would look like me? What does that say about her feelings for me?

I still have her every night all the same because I love her despite the hate and anger and violent jealously I am feeling, I want her more than ever. It is a sickness which is destroying me bit by bit. It has already destroyed my heart and now it is eating away at the rest of me.

I cannot take it anymore. I am fantasising about just killing myself now and ending all this pain.

My shrink says *I need to be in hospital again.*

I tell him *it is not possible.*

I am not leaving this demon alone. No way, I tell the shrink. I should have listened to him, I should have listened when he told me I would not find Kiára in this girl.

Now she has a dreamy look as she smiles at me in

a cloud of Coco Chanel. For a second, I see Kiára and then I see her expression which has no love in it, just a fake smile with contempt of me. She has been with a man. I can see the signs again. I grab her roughly and scream, "Who is it this time, you whore?" I raise my arm as if to strike her and she cries out and slides to the floor in a protective ball. I would not have hit her but just threatening to is terrible. She is turning me into something monstrous as we fall off the precipice together still fighting as we go.

Her contempt turns to fear and she says, "I don't know, I don't know him. I got into his car. I don't know why I do it. I hate myself for doing it, but we had safe sex." She looks up at me.

Oh, that's okay then, Lilla. It's okay if you're having safe sex. I am not going to get an STD then, so everything is okay.

I guess I have to be grateful she has the tiny scrap of consideration to use condoms with these people. These faceless, nameless men who fuck my wife. I don't know if it is better she doesn't care for them, doesn't know them. I believe it is. She is not leaving me for a meaningful lover which I would actually go crazy over. I would drag her across the world to stop her doing that.

She is having cold, passionless sex with men she never sees more than once. It is dangerous and I am worried about her safety. It is as though everything she is doing is reckless. The going out and getting into men's cars, the binge drinking. She is again offered help by my shrink who thinks she is deeply troubled and pills alone will not solve it. But she refuses.

After she admits that she hates what she is doing, she doesn't understand it, she wants to stop, I am angry. "Stop then, Lilla, just stop fucking around!" I shout. "You are my wife. Mine. And now you have been around half the men in Budapest. What part of your wedding vows did you forget? You are despicable. You make me sick! You should be getting paid for all this, it would be more honest!"

I scream at her and she covers her face with her hands.

"István, mama, please stop," Natalija has been listening and runs crying back into her room. I chase her and try to stop her tears. *My little girl. God forgive me if I damage her by what she has seen.*

"Is she leaving again?" asks Natalija. "What did I do?"

"Baby, you did nothing wrong. She loves you. It is me she hates. She is not leaving, I promise. We are just having some trouble right now."

I haul Lilla off the floor where she is sitting like a broken doll, some discarded toy I once loved and grew bored of. I push her into the bedroom and then into the shower and scrub her with a rough brush and some exfoliating shower gel as if I can get rid of her cheating as I tell her what Natalija said to me. "You are not just breaking me, Lilla. You are breaking that little girl's heart."

The brush must hurt her but she doesn't protest, just lets me scrub away the other man's scent or I can't touch her. She stands and takes her punishment and then I wrap her in a freshly laundered towel. She is not even drunk. She can't even use alcohol as an excuse.

Christmas and we are both so messed up even Natalija notices. Despite her toys and our pretence she asks *what's wrong, did she do something?*

Lilla scoops her up and says, "No, sweet lovely girl. Let's go and read you some of your new books." She leaves me sitting at the table with the remains of the dinner.

I put my head on the table and cry and cry. The

world is falling apart. I want to put it all back together. I want to so much.

I am taking her to Italy for the two weeks I have to be in conferences in early January. I am not having her cheating in my goddamn bed and she has enough holiday leave from work to take. She is happy that I say we are going to Italy but for once not so happy when we will be taking Natalija. "Natalija will be in our hotel room, why can't we just leave her with the au pair?" Lilla demands.

We are leaving Levente because although I hate leaving him, he would suffer just as much maternal deprivation with heartless Lilla who does nothing for him and he probably thinks the au pair is his mother by now. What a fucked up marriage this is.

"Because you cold hearted woman, she is a little girl and you are supposed to be her mother now. And your son; I am not bringing him because you will neglect him all day and he is better off with the au pair. She is going to be caring for him at night as well thanks to your neglect. He won't even know you when he is older," I say to her disgusted at the woman she has turned into.

Lilla says nothing as she knows I am right. She just doesn't want to have sex in the shower, I can't see why else she is miserable about having to take Natalija. We argue and I tell her *she doesn't want Natalija stopping her going around the whole of Rome and all the men whilst I am in conferences all day.*

She takes Natalija's hand as we go into the airport but she is still sulking about this whole trip.

Damn her to Hell.

We are in a pretty hotel and she can speak a little Italian but it is all lost on her. In the airbus from the airport she ignores the eternal city while Natalija is in love with this place already.

I vowed never to take her to conferences again but the thought of her with random men in my apartment is much worse than her scratching and biting me every night when Natalija is asleep.

I get a call on my cell phone when I am on lunch at the conference only on the second day we are there. They are gabbling in Italian and I say *please, I do not speak the language, I am sorry*.

In heavily accented English a man's voice says, "We have your wife with the police. She is arrested. She jumped into Trevi fountain. This is not allowed. She says she has no money to pay. You must pay the fine."

I am mad and when I arrive at the cop shop, Lilla is sitting there all angelic with Natalija on her knees. Lilla is wrapped in a blanket and she holds Natalija tight to stop her shivering.

"I saw it in that film *La Dolce Vita*," she says to me dreamily. "I didn't know it was illegal, I am really sorry. It was cold."

It is January, you stupid girl. Of course it would be fucking cold.

I am so mad as I pay the big fine.

My thoughts are hot like a red bubbling volcano and I think back to when she asked me *'If I betrayed you, would you kill me like Carmen?'*

We walk out of the cop shop and although Natalija is there I grab Lilla by the shoulders and scream at her, "Are you out of your fucking mind?"

Natalija starts to cry, "I am so cold, István. The water was freezing. She made us jump in."

Lilla just looks at me. There is nothing in her expression. I push her into the taxi I asked to wait for us and we go back to the hotel.

I tell Natalija we need to go to reception and I order Lilla to wait in the hotel room. "Sit there and don't do anything and I will be back in 5 minutes."

The manager agrees to let Natalija sit with him for 10 minutes. I tell him I have some real problems with my wife and I need to talk to her alone. He says to take as long as I need.

When I go back in the room Lilla is sitting on the bed unmoved, the same stupid vacant expression in her eyes.

I want to beat her just to get a reaction out of this stupid girl. Right now I do not know what I saw in her. Apart from her stunning beauty but she is as empty and vacant as a plastic doll as she sits looking at me with those large dark eyes and black lashes. An unfeeling doll.

I actually hate her so much I am afraid of what I will do if I spend one more day with her. I will beat her.

I look at Lilla who just gazes at me. I want to hit her so hard and that's when I realise I can't do this anymore. She is hurting me and messing up my work.

"Lilla, you need to leave, I have my apartment keys and I do not want you there. You are affecting my work now and I cannot have that. You have clothes with you here. Take these euros and get your flight back to Budapest or wherever you want. But you are not coming back to my apartment. You do not care about our son and you just jumped into the fucking fountain with my little girl in January. You are sick, you need help. Go and get help and then call me but I cannot deal with this any longer." I start throwing her clothes in her suitcase.

"You're throwing me out," she is now showing shock and disbelief. "You don't want me anymore? I thought you loved me."

"I can't take it anymore, Lilla. Maybe we can talk if you are in Hungary once I get back but you need to show me you are seeing a shrink or getting help. But you need to get out of my life right now. I am not saying it is over, I just need you gone for now. I am at breaking point," I tell her coldly. I finish packing all her clothes and all her possessions in her suitcase as she keeps whining on about she will change, please don't do this.

She is begging and pleading she is sorry and I have to prise her fingers off the doorframe and throw her out of the room. It hurts like Hell as I drag her down the corridor and my heart is stabbing me when she is like this but I just cannot deal with this girl anymore. I will hurt her if I have another incident. I will really hurt her.

Natalija will be upset with me for a while but I am here to work and Lilla is destroying me and I am afraid of what I might do to her if this kind of situation happens again. I escort her out the fire exit into the street with her bag and all the time she is pleading and telling me she loves me but it is just too little too late. I push her into a taxi and tell the driver not to stop until he reaches the airport.

Lilla is trying to get out but I shove her back in and shout, "I do not want you here! Get the Hell away from me. I don't love you. Goodbye, Lilla."

And her expression as the car drives away haunts me. *Stunned, heartbroken, helpless.*

I go to fetch Natalija and thank the hotel manager.

"Where's mama?" says Natalija.

"She had to go back to Hungary, baby. Her mother is not well. She said she loves you very much but she has to see her mother," I tell her.

I expected more emotion from Natalija but she just says, "But she still loves me? Because she is strange now, István. Is she sick too?"

"She is not feeling so well but she loves you very much," I tell her. "All the time."

And I know she does.

I have had to pay some extortionate rate for an

Italian au pair organised by the manager. He knows of a very good lady but it means getting a taxi early, trekking across the city in the frenzied Roman traffic with Natalija and leaving her there then rushing to the conference every day.

I get no end of missed calls on my cell phone, texts pleading with me to talk. But I cannot think of Lilla. I have to push her aside. It is easier now I have thrown her out than when she left me as her callous disregard of our son has really made me hate her at times. And I am so stretched with attending conferences and caring for my daughter I am just too tired. I know I should call her back and just see if she is okay. She is obviously sick.

I should call her just to say I am not so angry. Her behaviour was stupid but we can sort everything out. After a few days, I am calmer and clearer. It is not too late. I should reassure her that she is sick, that I do love her and I was angry when I told her I didn't and if she goes to the shrink, we can work things out.

But I am so tired and so busy the two weeks go quickly for me.

I wish to God I had called her, told her that I still loved her but she needed to get help. That I hadn't told her this was the end, just I cannot deal with any more right now. I wish I had told her how much I loved her despite her crazy behaviour, her cheating and her lying.

FRAGMENTS

When I am back in the apartment, that's when it hits me. I feel it. Or the lack of it. Cruel damaged Lilla. *She is not here*. There is no magical cloud of Coco Chanel hovering in the air. She hasn't been here since we left together 2 weeks ago. I have bought her a few Italian dresses in the airport I wanted to give her. The apartment seems so empty without her. I want her back immediately. I resolve to talk to her after work tomorrow. I have to work it out with her. She needs medical help.

I expect to see her in work at the dental surgery the next day. I do not know how I will deal with it but she is not there. I ask has she resigned.

"No she is in hospital, her mother called us. We are not sure when she will be back," says the practice manager.

"What is wrong, do you know? I am sorry but we argued and we decided it was best she returned to Hungary ahead of me."

"Her mother just said she was sick, I am sorry but that's all I know," the manager tells me. "Maybe call the hospital before you start, István."

I want to call but I have no privacy or time that day to call until I get home.

When I do call her mother that evening she is shouting as me. God, Ágnes is a witch.

When I get sense out of her and ask what is wrong she says Lilla took an overdose.

"I found her surrounded by bottles and bottles of pills. Your fault, you did this. You ruined her life so she tried to end it," she tells me.

I am frantic and I have to see her but Ágnes says to stay away, stay away from the hospital.

"She does not want to see you, István," she says. "Never, ever again. Spend life on your own."

I take her word for it. I send a huge bouquet of red roses to the hospital. I write in the card:

'Lilla, I am so sorry. Please get well. If you want to see me, you can. Your István'.

When she is back in work two weeks later, I don't know what emotion I am feeling. I ask her did she get my flowers. She can't look at me and she nods. She looks beautiful but so pale and fragile. I tell her *I would like to see her if she wants, but please call me first and we can have some time maybe on a weekend.* She just nods again without looking at me. I know she must be suffering from depression combined with all her other problems. I put my hand on hers as no one is around and she is setting up the reception for the day and she looks at me and those lovely brown eyes are full of sadness.

"I had no idea, Lilla, no idea you felt so bad," I whisper and I go to get changed into my dental uniform. "I'm so sorry," I say. I don't know if she heard this last bit. What I mean is *I am so sorry I drove you to do this. Your behaviour was crazy in Rome, but I should have seen through it. I should not have pushed you away and sent you back on a plane. I am responsible. I should have learned from Kiára. I should have helped you. If you had died from your overdose I would not have been able to live with myself.*

She sits on the apartment doorstep waiting for me. This dark angel. Why didn't she go in? She knows Kata will be there looking after the children. Maybe she felt she couldn't. Maybe she thought I would throw her out again. I do not know if I want her inside. She stands up as I get to the steps and says, "My liver is damaged. All those pills."

"I am really sorry to hear that, Lilla. I hope you get

better," I say and I mean it.

"Can I come in?"

"No, I am sorry but I had an exhausting day and right now I don't know how I am feeling, Lilla. I need time to think and I know that if I let you back in you will smash my heart up even more. You will hurt Natalija and your hatred of me and our son hurts me even if you don't care," I say.

"Please, let me talk to you," she says. She looks at me with her beautiful face but this time I will not give in.

"I'm sorry," I say. "You need to give me a few days, Lilla. Then come over. Call me, just not tonight. Look, just give me a few more days. Tonight I am exhausted."

"I love you," she says as I pass her.

I stop and I kiss her cheek. "I do want to see you, Lilla. But not tonight. Please don't do anything stupid. I said things I didn't mean when I was angry in Rome. I shouldn't have said what I did so please just wait a few days and we can sort something out. Okay? Promise me, Lilla? For me," I say more gently taking her hand. "Baby, I promise we will work it out, just tell me you are safe tonight."

She agrees she is not going to do anything reckless and I watch her walk away.

I want to let her in. I want to turn around and stop us both hurting and hold her but tonight I can't.

I am not feeling soft tonight. It will have to wait.

I cannot take any more when I am in the surgery working late that week and everyone else has left and I have my key to lock the building. The operation was more complex so I needed to sit in the office and finish off some paperwork to come down after the stress. I am so tired and I go to change in the locker room. I hear voices which I find strange as I locked the front door after my patient and the dental assistant left, but maybe the cleaners are here. I walk into the room and my heart seems to fall out of my chest and shatters into a thousand pieces on the floor. I see András and Lilla and she has an expression of ecstasy on her face as he is taking her against the wall still in his dental whites although his pants are round his ankles. It makes me scream out loud, an animal cry. András. Now it is real, now it is someone I know, the junior dentist she flirted with in front of me before. András is terrified and trying to pull up his pants and he swears *this is the first time, she wanted him, he knew he shouldn't* and I silence his protest as I smack him in the face knocking him over and I kick him in his balls. His pants are still round his ankles. He lies there groaning. *Good*, I think. *Bastard.*

He should have told her, 'No, you are married to István. You love him. You have a life with him. You have a child with him. We all work together. It is too dangerous.'

He should have stopped her. She's just a fucked up girl. She tried to kill herself a couple of weeks ago and this idiot is helping her self-destruct more than ever. I am so mad I could kill him. Not that he knows about Lilla. He just sees a beautiful sultry girl who appears so cool and together.

Would she have done it if I had let her in the other night when she was waiting on my apartment steps?

I just don't know. I don't know with her. I should have let her in. She had suffered enough.

Lilla looks at me with sadness, her dark eyes full of 'forgive me, I love you, I don't know what I am doing'. It makes a change from contempt as she pulls down her dress and adjusts her clothes. I see the condom wrapper on the floor and I am so angry I pick it up and stuff it in Lilla's mouth until she gags. This is the final insult. She spits out the wrapper and starts her whining, "Forgive me, I couldn't stop, I didn't....."

I tell her we need to go for a drive and I grab her arm tightly and we step over András who is holding his soon to be black eye. I have nothing to say to him. He is lucky I don't kick him harder on the way out.

I just tell him, "Make sure you lock up after your shag. You have keys don't you?"

"Yes," he groans.

"You have just signed your own death warrant, András," I say.

My Carmen, my lovely Carmen. You and your cheating heart. I really could murder you right now.

Lilla is pleading on the way out *she never did it with him before, she doesn't care about him.*

But he works here and this is too much. He is not one of the nameless, faceless men who disappear into the dark heart of the city but someone junior to me and he has just fucked my wife, my prize, my possession. It could easily happen again. And again. How much longer do I torture myself?

"Get in the fucking car, Lilla," I order her. Then I press the door lock button. There are childproof locks so she will not be able to get out.

I have the car as I was going to drive into the downtown to buy something, we can talk as I drive. I accelerate out of the car park with a screeching of tyres and shoot a red light.

Lilla says, "Please slow down, István."

I am speeding into the night faster and faster not knowing what is real any longer and Lilla is pleading with me to slow down but I am determined as I take the road at 120kmph, then 140kmph into the hills of the XII district. I do not know where I am going. Lilla reaches for her seatbelt but I push her hands away to stop her fastening it.

"Please István. Don't be like this. We can work everything out," she says.

"No we can't, baby. You ruin me. You are so bad for me," I tell her.

I need to get back to the children but I am out of control right now.

"Baby we are finished," I say as I move into the centre of the road and accelerate harder round the bends. "We can't carry on. Not now, not after what you did. I can't forgive you. I can't ever forgive you for what you did."

"Please slow down, István. We don't have to die," Lilla says in desperation. She starts to cry but I do not care for her frozen tears.

"You broke my heart Lilla. You disappeared when I needed you most that April and didn't care. I would have never let you go for a day without me and you lied to me and cheated and smashed my heart to fragments. I loved you so much I could die for you. We can't live now, baby. We can only die together," I say.

I am crying too but I am driving faster in the darkness.

"István, think of Natalija, all alone. I have said I am sorry a thousand times; I wish every day I could take it back. How can you leave your little girl? And Levente, you wanted him so much. I am sorry I did what I did. I regret it so much, everything."

Treacherous Carmen. I could kill you now.

"Please, don't do this," Lilla touches my hand and tries to hold it but I close my fist in anger.

"You love me and I can learn to love, I can, I promise. I am so sorry I have been so stupid, please forgive me," she says.

"I need help, I promise I will go to the shrink and I will go every day if I have to just don't do this, just stop the car if only for today and I swear to you I will change."

I hesitate as she is speaking as though she means it and think of Natalija and Levente; they are my life and I have to get back to them, but I have already taken the bend too fast. I look at Lilla for a second and see her beauty, her face now gentle looking at me with hope, the Kiára I searched for and found again.

Wait, we need more time, we can start again.......if only.....

I imagine that .....I let go of the wheel and grab hold of my Lilla as the lights of the oncoming car meet us on the blind corner. No one else can have her. She will be mine forever now.

The windscreen shatters into a million stars glittering and beautiful, these fragments and this is the last thought I have as we fly through it or it flies towards us, a milky way in the darkness. Through the blackness there are only beautiful lights.

But I cannot bring myself to do it. Just me and Lilla and I would do it. Right now I would kill us both. But for Natalija and Levente I will not. I slow down and I am shaking with the thought of what if we met another car on those bends. I drive back down to the city and I cast Lilla out in the downtown and she is crying. I have to get out of the car to pull her hands off the door as she is clinging on so hard and drag her out which breaks my heart and I tell her, "For God's sake do not try to kill yourself again, you've damaged your body enough."

I get back in and I drive on wiping the tears away, resolving I will get over her.

She runs after my car shouting and I have to ignore her and drive home, burning inside.

I was so close, so close to killing us both. We are killing each other with our love and hate.

The first thing I do in the morning is have András

fired. It isn't difficult. He wasn't that great anyway and I tell the practice manager *I caught him having sex with one of the patients as I was finishing my shift. In the toilet of all places.* This is Hungary and there are not many medical ethics. I dated Kiára when she was my patient but a junior doctor who has sex in the bathroom with a patient is done for.

Even if he didn't do it. András doesn't argue. He knows his life is not worth living as he knows of my reputation. He is afraid of me. He also knows my patients consist of many senior figures such as lawyers and cops and he is afraid of what I might do. He has heard rumours that I am involved with the Hungarian mafia. This is totally untrue but I have overheard some staff say it and I would not correct them because I do not care what they think. As long as they respect me, I don't give a flying fuck.

But I will not come into work and see his face knowing he screwed my wife. Or is she my ex-wife. Whatever.

Lilla watches him leave and looks at me.

Her desperation is touching but I really don't love her right now, I hate her. I am sorry that she is pain, obvious pain from her liver damage after her overdose but she pushed me too far for too long.

Each day I become stronger and she is weaker. She sends me pleading texts, she finds any chance in work to talk to me and beg me but my resolve is strong. I am feeling better without her.

She starts sending me goddamn gifts and cards telling me how much she loves me.

Tacky chocolate hearts and red roses and other childish romantic shit.

I take them home and give them to Natalija. I just tell her they are gifts from Lilla.

Lilla says she wants to see our son which I can't believe. She says she wants to see Natalija which I find credible enough. She does care for her very much but I am reluctant to let this woman back into my life again. But the little girl has been upset without Lilla and for the sake of my daughter I agree. But I hate her for neglecting Levente so much already; her own blood. I walk back to the apartment with her and tell her I will let her get on with it. I will go out. I know if I stay I will want her too much. I am not over her, not by a long way.

"Please, please don't go," she says. "I wanted to talk to you."

"I have a date," I say. I don't but I just want to be cruel. "And she's smoking hot, baby."

She is so easy to hurt now. I can feel her sad gaze on my back as I leave.

I return 2 hours later wondering if she has changed the locks, wondering if she has done something crazy. I think I should not have left her alone, I should have paid Kata to stay longer.

But Natalija is asleep and Levente too and Lilla is nowhere to be found. I am so afraid she has done something stupid like tried to kill herself and I will find her unconscious in my bedroom.

She is in my room except undressed and in my goddamn bed.

"Get out," I tell her.

"I love you. I put Levente to bed too. I gave him his bottle."

What do you want a gold medal? For the first time in his life you actually touch him? Then I remember when I cheated on her I left her all night with him and she took care of him. I am full of conflicting emotions; wanting her so badly and hating her at the same time.

"Get out!" I shout and pull away the duvet. I try not to look at her body in her red silk underwear but I am weak. She grabs my hand and begs me to join her.

"It is our bed, my love," she says.

I am not weak, I am fucking weak. And my face is in her hair, I taste her skin, kiss her neck and I try to think 'this is just sex'. She wraps herself around me. I desperately want to just curl up with her and hold her all night but I tell her, "Now get your shit, and get the Hell out," like I mean it.

I shove her out of bed hard and she says, "I thought you loved me," so pathetically as she lies on the bedroom floor.

I want to tell her I do. I love her so much. I am just fucking it up. We both are.

"I thought I did too, baby," I say and I turn over. "Shut the door on your way out."

I hear her crying as she gets dressed so I put the pillow over my head. I will not let this demon back into my life.

Easy to say when I have to face her in work every day, when her texts carry on and I can't bear to change my number or block her because I do love her. But she has savaged me, lied, cheated and cut me up and I know I could let her in again and she will turn. She will turn into that demon girl with such contempt of me.

And the other problem is she is still legally married to me. Even if I divorce her which I could never bear to do in a million years, Natalija still needs to see her and Levente too. So every weekend I have agreed she can spend time at the house but she is so treacherous that it could all be an act to pretend she has changed.

And I have my needs. I hate my weakness but when the children are asleep I need sex and it is her I want not some random forgettable woman in a bar. I want Lilla's body and this time I can't shove her out of the bed when I am done. I need to hold her and sleep wrapped around her. She is complaining her liver is hurting and I do not know if she is lying but I am not that cruel. And she feels so warm in my arms.

But she is obviously in pain as the next day I look in the mirror as I get up first and see her hold her side as she gets out of bed. She has damaged her liver and she tells me the doctors are hoping it will recover but there is no guarantee. I am sorry as I know me throwing her out of the hotel in Rome led to this but instead of saying 'Sorry, I was cruel', I come out with:

"Why did you take an overdose? What a stupid thing to do."

"You cut your goddamn wrists and I had to patch you up, remember? That was the stupidest thing you could have done. You could have ended your career," she says. "And you are old enough to know better. I'm just a fucked up teenager, what's your excuse?"

Yes I fucking remember my wrists and it makes me feel ill. And I do know I could have ended my career. I do not want to be reminded of this.

"Well you should understand then," she says. "Maybe you will wake up to me and I will be dead and then you'll be happy."

It is a direct reference to Kiára. She has not thought out this throwaway remark but it cuts into me deeper than anything.

This little bitch hasn't changed. I grab her wrist. "Alright, get out. Get the Hell out. How dare you refer to Kiára in that way. I loved her, I would have done anything. She had a heart unlike you. Yours is frozen and dead." I drag her out of bed.

"Hey take it easy," she says. "I'm sorry, I didn't mean to insult Kiára. I really didn't, István. It was stupid to say that. I just always feel you loved her and not me."

"Just go, Lilla, just fuck off. She earned my love and you with your lying and cheating and cold behaviour do not. I just like fucking you too much to let you go."

Fragments

I slap her ass hard, like the child she is and shove her into her clothes. She looks at me with those big eyes full of hurt.

"And Lilla, I won't wake up to you lifeless and cold because you are already dead, with your frozen heart. You are already dead, baby." I turn away from her. I can't bear to see the pain in her eyes.

I am nasty and have reduced everything we have or had to cold meaningless sex. And I know it isn't just that. I am behaving like a complete bastard to punish her for hurting me.

"Can I come and see the children tomorrow?" she asks in a small voice as she is about to leave.

"Okay, it's Sunday. But you are not to stay over and that is final," I say through the bedclothes.

"Now go, Lilla. I need to sleep."

I hear the front door close and I am not feeling good at all. I want her here next to me.

Natalija has ice skating in the morning. She is only 5 and wants to be an Olympic gold medallist. I am happy about that; she already has ambition. She started skating at 3 years old which is good, as young children have no fear on the ice. She is already competitive and wants to be the best in her class. She gets angry when she doesn't do well and I wonder if she is going to turn out like me, competitive and pushing everyone out of the way in the name of success. It is no bad thing.

So Lilla is left alone when I go to collect Natalija from the ice rink.

I tell her, "For God's sake, just do something useful. Bake some healthy cakes for Natalija, she will be hungry. I sent you on that cookery course and you can still only make cakes, you useless girl. And if Levente wakes up, can you see to him."

I am being deliberately cruel and I don't really

want to talk to her. But the resolve I had to keep her out of my bed tonight has already splintered. She looks so beautiful today in her tight black dress, I know I would need to be struck by lightning to keep my hands off her. I will just have to be cold and unloving afterwards and go to sleep.

I have not had any episodes for a while and my mind is clearer, stronger without her. I want to keep it that way.

Lilla just says *fine she will stay here and make the cakes*. But she is hurt, really hurt by my vicious words. I look at her for a minute as she reaches into the fridge and she looks so sad and so beautiful, I just want to go over and hold her and be loving towards her.

But I don't.

At the ice rink, Natalija is not fine. She is sitting alone on a bench, dark and angry. The skating teacher says she thinks Natalija is not right for her group. Today she told them all she was prettier and better than all of them. 'I am the best skater here,' she said.

She is exceptional for her age but she seems to be unable to get on with other children. *The only thing we can do, is give her private tuition. It is more expensive but Natalija cannot carry on in a group. She seems troubled. Is something wrong at home? She has been very angry for a while now. She says she has a new brother, is that the problem?*

"No," I say. "My wife gives Natalija all the attention. Natalija is a spoilt little princess."

I look at Natalija, already devastatingly good-looking but her expression is full of black angry thoughts. She reminds me of myself.

"My wife and I are having small troubles. It isn't that. I think she just wants to be the best skater. She wants to win. She is just very competitive."

I know the whole Lilla situation has not helped. But it can't be the only problem. I take her home and she is quiet, moody. "I'm not mad at you, baby. But you know you can't have group classes anymore, the teacher said we give you private lessons."

"Good," she says. "Good. I can't stand those idiots in my group. I really wanted to kick one of them today with my skate."

I tell her *she can't do that, she can't go around behaving like a sociopath.*

"What is a sociopath?" she asks me.

I want to say 'like Lilla, like me' but this is not a good idea.

Someone who hates other people.

"Oh," she says.

Then she suddenly comes out with, "I know why you lock your bedroom door at night."

"Why, Natalija?" I ask as I look at the road ahead.

"Sex. You like sex. I heard you telling Lilla that's why she is there. You said, 'I love sex with you', but Lilla is so sad now. Maybe she doesn't like the sex," Natalija laughs and looks out of the window.

I don't know what to say. All I can say is, "Natalija, Lilla does like sex and how do you know all about this anyway? Are you listening at doors?"

Natalija just smiles at me. "I'm smart for my age, right? Is sex good? Can I do it with you?"

She laughs.

"Natalija that is enough. Sex is for adults. And it is never for me and you. You are my little girl. You are too young to ask me about sex. Ask me in 8 years time and I will talk to you, but sex is for adults who love each other never fathers and daughters. Natalija you shouldn't even think about sex. Just don't get too smart. Stick to figure skating and you won't go wrong. When you are older you will understand boys and men are after only one thing. It's depressing," I say. "Don't grow up too fast, darling. I mean it."

"But you love me, right?" she says in such an adult way it hurts me.

"Yes, but it isn't that kind of love, baby. You will always be my little girl."

I am shocked that my daughter has just asked me about sex and I hope it isn't because Lilla has been talking to her. It might just be natural childish curiosity but the question, 'can I do it with you?' disturbs me as I can't imagine Natalija thinking of this by herself. It is not the kind of question she would come out with. Lilla has said something.

I know Lilla has had to grow up too fast, I just pray she hasn't been telling Natalija too much, she is unbalanced enough to do it. I can hear her now in my head telling my daughter about sex. "Your father is a sex-obsessed animal, Natalija. That's all he wants me for, sex. He wants every woman just for sex."

And Natalija would look at her seriously, not understanding but remembering the entire conversation.

I have a horrible fear Natalija will suddenly announce in a public place, "My daddy is good at sex."

And the cops would be over, I would be arrested, all because Lilla has been talking inappropriately to my daughter.

My fault. All of this mess.

DAMAGE

Lilla has agreed to attend the shrink with me. I say it is mainly for her. We are not going to go anywhere unless she does. If she wants to live with me again, she has to show she is working through her problems. She agrees sadly as she knows I am winning in this crazy power game. We hurt, we love, we hate and we go back in a spiral of pain.

In the car on the way there I ask her, "Lilla, have you been talking to Natalija about sex? She knows a Hell of a lot for her age."

Lilla is silent for a minute and says, "I think I might have said something. She asks me questions, you know."

"Please don't, Lilla. If she needs to ask a question, she can ask me. You are not in a good frame of mind and I really think you have said more than you should to a little girl. The next time I will end up being accused of something. Maybe you are trying to do that. Maybe you want to break this family apart. I don't know what your game is, Lilla."

She just looks out of the window twirling her hair. I want to slap her if she has been malicious but I can't prove what she did or didn't say. I don't know who this angel or demon is anymore.

We sit side by side in the shrink's office. Lilla looks as though she has no emotion whatsoever. He asks her gently to describe if she can the moment her father died.

"I was 12 years old when my father jumped into he path of a train in front of me. I was close to my father. He was a doctor but he was sad a lot of the time. I never got on with my mother but my father loved me. It was a January day and he decided we would go out together although I knew he wasn't feeling well. He had promised to take me to the shops and buy me a gift. We were in Eger at the time, visiting our relatives. He told me to stand back as a train was approaching and I thought he would stand back too but at the last minute he let go of my hand and he jumped in front of the train. It was one of the express trains passing through the station. I heard screams from other people on the platform, I heard a crunching which I know were his bones and then he was chopped up all over the track. He was dead. His eyes were open. I could not stop looking. The train driver was sitting on the platform with his head in his hands and people were screaming but I just stood there frozen to the place I was standing in and I stared and stared at his body until some ladies led me away. And then I didn't talk to anyone for 2 years. Not one word. Not even to my mother." Lilla looks directly at the shrink as if she is reading a novel about an incident which happened to someone else.

"How do you feel now Lilla, is it upsetting you, we can stop or pause if you need to," says the shrink gently.

"Nothing, I feel nothing," says Lilla. "I cannot feel. Most of the time I cannot feel. I feel angry but not because of that."

I look at her and she is staring straight ahead, no emotions in her face good or bad.

"Do you relive the moment, I mean does it suddenly feel like you are back in that time and you can see it all over again?" he asks her.

"Yes, at times. I am not thinking of it and it will suddenly be there in my head. As though it just emerges without warning and I am that 12 year old again and I can see it as clearly as I can see you in the room now," she says.

I am distressed enough hearing about it. I reach for her hand and she lets me. Not because she needs me, more because I need to.

He asks her to fill in a questionnaire and adds up her score.

The shrink asks to speak to me alone after the session. He tells me *Lilla is suffering from severe post-traumatic stress disorder. She is depersonalised. She doesn't feel real. She cannot connect with people. He can work with her but it will take a long, long time.*

He tells me *her anger, her reckless behaviour, her cheating with all these men, her inability to love me or her son is all part of the condition. It is very hard to get through to someone like that. It is not something many people can do.*

I tell him *the only time she shows emotion is when she is treated cruelly. Show her love, shower her with gifts and she doesn't care. She has cheated all over Budapest, she has broken my heart and she has made my bipolar disorder a thousand times worse. Right now I have thrown her out and she is pleading and begging me to come back. It is the only time I have any control.*

"She is very damaged and it has gone on a long time, it is hard to help someone who refuses help. But she is here today. She has started to talk. And I believe she is not cheating because she wants to, it is all a pattern of self-destructive behaviour," he tells me.

Well it doesn't help me when she says it's the last time she cheats and then goes and does it again.

"I really don't know if I can love her as I can't trust her after all she put me through," I tell him.

"She took an overdose, she damaged her liver. I can't really suggest what you should do as you have your own illness but she needs love. As you know her mother didn't love her enough," he says.

"And still doesn't. You said she didn't even send flowers to Lilla after she had your son. That she never wants to see her grandchild. She didn't call once."

Again I think *how could Lilla's mother be so heartless?* But then I remember so much Lilla has done to hurt me.

"I caught her fucking one of the junior dentists," I tell him. "She says she feels nothing for these men but I walked in and saw her. How can I trust her after that? She left me for a month with no note, nothing, a year ago. I thought I would never see her again. She smashed my heart into millions of fragments," I say.

"Some people have relationships which are destructive. I can't tell you what to do, István. I can only tell you what the problem is because I know you will do what you want to do in the end. It is just a question of whether you love this girl enough to work through the problems because her recklessness will not stop overnight. And you are sick too. If she makes you ill, you have to question what you're doing."

She does make me ill, no doubt about it.

The shrink has given me the phone number of an elderly man who had witnessed great suffering under the Soviet occupation. He is one of his patients but the man had said any help he could offer to someone suffering post-traumatic stress disorder, he would. He was feeling better after 2 years of seeing the shrink and he wanted to help anyone else in a similar state. Groups are not the answer for Lilla, the doctor tells me. He thinks she will not talk in a group but as well as seeing him for therapy, she might be helped if she can call this elderly man. She also needs medication. He writes a prescription for anti-depressants and benzos.

"I know you are worried, István, after Kiára but I think Lilla's depression is more reactive. It has definitely got worse after Levente but the main cause was her father's death which was not dealt with.

These pills will help her short-term but she can't take a high dose because she damaged her liver. I just hope it regenerates, for her and for you," he says as I am leaving.

Stupid selfish girl. She didn't think of me when she took her overdose. I am worried sick that she will not fully recover. Doesn't she know what she did to me? What would I say to Levente if she died? Your mother killed herself because of the way I treated her and your sister's mother also died and I could have stopped that too. The thoughts are horrendous. What will these children think when they can understand what really happened? They will blame me.

I expect Lilla to say she is not going back, she will not take the pills and she will not call the elderly man; she doesn't need any help. However, she agrees to take the treatment and the prescriptions and she takes the phone number of the man who has offered to speak to her.

So we carry on in our separate worlds. She still comes over at weekends. She stays in my bed. But only because I want her body; I am trying so hard not to love her. I am afraid of her and her damaged heart. She has agreed to see the shrink twice a week. I am paying. She has already called the man who offered to talk to her about post-traumatic stress disorder and she has started her medication. But I can't let her back for good. At least not yet. I need my space to clear my head.

It is late and someone won't stop ringing the goddamn bell. I look at the clock 01.22. Fucking Monday night and I need my sleep. I have to get up as it could be an emergency; maybe a neighbour, someone might be ill. I open the door and Lilla collapses into me and her face is bleeding; her lip split, a big cut over her eye and bruises round her neck. She cries.

"Oh God, Lilla," I pick her up and carry her to the bathroom to clean her face. I check her teeth but they are not damaged. "Lilla, what happened?"

"I was in someone's apartment, I don't know where, somewhere in the III district and he got nasty," she says.

"Lilla look at me," I take her face in my hands. "Baby, look at me. This stops right now. Right now. You stop this self-destructive behaviour. Do you want to wind up dead?"

"Why would you care, you threw me out?" she says wiping her face.

"This stops right here." I take off her coat and see she has bruises and bites all over her chest.

I carry her broken and pathetic into the bed and tell her, "Just sleep, sleep, you are safe now."

God, Lilla. What are you doing to yourself, to us? How can you do this?

And I feel such tenderness for this damaged girl. I really believe she has changed after this and I go away to a course in Munich feeling glad we resolved it and I call her every evening although we have very little to say to each other. I just think of Kiára as we talk and I think thoughts of Lilla that I would not have thought so crudely about Kiára, such as 'Lilla is such an amazing fuck.' I am looking forward to returning to her. We still have a chance. We can still have a good life.

But it is not only me who thinks this.

I am back on an earlier flight from Munich on the Saturday morning feeling happy to be seeing Lilla in my apartment. When I unlock the door, I hear sounds from the bedroom; at first I think she is actually talking to Levente as the au pair is not here today but I look in the nursery and he is asleep, Natalija is at her friend's house for the weekend. As I push open the door there she is; my false love, her eyes closed in ecstasy while she is being fucked in my bed.

I stand for a minute and just watch. Then her eyes open and she looks on in shock while the man oblivious keeps at it.

"You might want to finish your orgasm before you leave," I say.

He nearly dies of fright and starts stammering some apology as he staggers out of the bed, this young stud. I scoop up his clothes and I throw them out of the window. He leaps out of the room naked and out through the door to search for his clothes amongst the trees of the garden below. It could be comical but I have nothing to laugh about. I could have hit him but my anger is not with him.

I turn to Lilla.

This time I cannot hold back; *my bed, my kingdom, my fucking bed.* I hold up the empty condom wrapper and look at her and she looks so terrified she can't speak. I pin her to the bed and pull her head back by her hair so she looks at me with frightened eyes. I scream, "What part of your wedding vows did you forget?!"

She tries to say she didn't mean to, she loves me.

I tell her to, "Shut the fuck up or I will strangle you right here, right now."

I fuck her without even taking off my clothes thinking, 'this is the last time, the last time I do this' and hurt her as much as I can as I am blind with rage and as she is weeping and trying to say she is sorry this makes me even madder so I grab her by her hair and haul her out of our bed. I take off my belt and beat her with it. *God forgive me,* I think afterwards as she cries with every smack the leather makes on her flesh. She curls into a ball sobbing and begging me to stop. I beat her across her back and call her *a whore, a treacherous whore, I loved you, I loved you.* I am weeping as I say it. *My Carmen and you asked me to kill you if you betrayed me?*

"Get the Hell out and never ever come back here," I say turning away from her. "I can't look at you. I gave you a million chances. And my bed, Lilla, that is the biggest insult of all, you goddamn whore. And my son sleeping next door. I hate you. I hate you. If I look at you I will kill you. I let you in after you were beaten by some crazy fuck and this is how you repay me when I am away on work conferences. How could you?" I go into the bathroom so she doesn't see me crying as she gathers her clothes and I hear her crying softly as she leaves the apartment.

I am full of horror as I tear off the sheets from the bed and stuff them in the wash. I am in shock over beating her and what she has turned me into. I am in shock that her cheating took place in my own bed. I think this is the worst feeling. *Cheat, I know you do, but in my apartment? In my own goddamn bed?* I cannot face sleeping in that room tonight so I collapse on the sofa my mind churning in disgust; in disgust with her and disgust at myself.

And I was feeling sorry and let her back in because someone had beaten her on one of her sexual escapades. I cry angry tears.

I am relieved Kata is not here to see me in this state. Lilla must have sent her home because she was having company. Levente has been fed and changed. The demon actually did something for him. I hold him close to me and cry. "Your mother is the cruellest woman ever to exist," I tell him as he looks at me with big dark eyes. "She broke my heart."

After this I do not miss her at all for a few days as I am so angry. And I am horrified with myself for beating a woman like that, however much she had betrayed me. Beating her with my belt like an absolute sadist. *How could we ever love again after that? How could she forgive me?* She does not call and I think it is best. I immerse myself in my work and begin to go back to the 12 hour days of before. I don't want to think. I want to be tired from work and forget about the lust which eats away at my brain when I think about sex. I still miss that. I am missing out on the children by working these long hours but I have to now; my dentistry is the only thing I have to anchor me to the ground.

I tell the practice manager *Lilla is not well.* Again I am covering up.

But she has handed in her resignation, didn't I know?

She isn't well, I tell the manager. *I know she quit but I hope to persuade her to come back.*

This woman, Linda looks at me and tells me *Lilla came in upset first thing this morning and said I had thrown her out and she could no longer continue with her job as she would have to face me every day.*

I feel sick that people know. Although Linda looks sorry and says *she hopes we can work it out and she promises me if I can talk to Lilla, she will happily take her back. She is very good at her job.*

"I am so sorry, István," she says. And she means it.

However, two of the dental assistants were in before me this morning and overheard the conversation between Lilla and the manager. I hear them as I get changed alone in the locker room. The stupid girls are in the staff bathroom and didn't hear me walk into the locker room.

"Yeah, she left him. She was crying and saying he threw her out."

"What a bastard. He is a real woman hater, isn't he?"

"Yes, I feel sorry for her now. I didn't like her, thought she always looked at us as if she was too good for us but the poor girl is half his age, more I think as he's older than he looks."

"She is stuck with him though. She will have to go back. She had a baby in July, remember?"

"I guess she got herself knocked up pretty fast just for a share of his money. He's loaded."

They laugh and one says, "Would you sleep with him if he asked you?"

"I would if I met him in a bar. When I started working here I thought he was gorgeous. Then I realised shame, because he is an arrogant asshole."

"I think I'd like him to screw me just to see what it was like, to see if he's as good in bed as he obviously thinks he is. He really loves himself. King of the bedroom!"

Both of them laugh.

"And you know why he wears white jeans instead of loose trousers with his dental uniform?"

"Why?"

"Because he is so sex crazed he walks around with a permanent erection; his jeans hide it!"

The bitches both screech with laughter.

"His poor wife. She must have been exhausted. I bet that's why she left."

The bathroom door is slightly ajar.

I go and stand there and look as Anikó and Viktória put on their make-up. Anikó senses something and turns around. She is ghostly pale. "Doktor Úr, good morning," she says.

"Is everything alright, Doktor Úr?" says Viktória who is clutching the washbasin in fear.

I step into the bathroom and close the door.

Random thoughts go through my head. Would I fuck these girls? Would I grope them, would I slap their asses and ask for a blow job? I vaguely remember making some inappropriate comments when I was in my manic episodes.

Viktória maybe but she is a dumb blonde. Anikó is

dark but lumpy and shapeless.

"Do you know what happens to girls who gossip about people?"

"Noooo..." they both say.

It is easy to scare these girls. It is even easier when they know how disposable they are. Employment contracts in Hungary count for shit especially the lower down the food chain you are.

"My wife is coming back soon; we are just having a break. Viktória, I wouldn't have lowered myself to fuck you even after a bottle of pálinka. I wouldn't even grope you, not because I can't but because I really couldn't be bothered although if you gave me a blow job I guess it would be okay and Anikó, you are just a misshapen lump of a girl I would need to cover your head with a paper bag to even get close. You really are ugly. But I could take it off and you could give me a quick blow job if I shut my eyes."

I laugh and I am standing right over them now and they are virtually sitting in the sink. It must freak them out as I am wearing nothing but a pair of boxer shorts as I was just getting changed ready for surgery. I am almost touching these stupid girls who look so frightened.

"But I am glad you say I am handsome and arrogant. So we are both right there," I give them a cobra smile. "I hope you are going to keep your mouths shut now, girls because it would be a real shame if you had to look for another workplace, wouldn't it?"

"I won't say anything, I promise," says Viktória.

"Lilla's a lovely girl," says Anikó too afraid to think of anything else to say.

"She's beautiful, that's why I am married to her and not girls like you. I throw her out though if she is a bad girl, which is why she won't be here for a bit. But when she's good and obedient, I'll take her back.

See, I call the shots. In work and out of it. And she had a child for me and not to get hold of my money. You are wrong about Lilla. She is not a dumb gold-digger like any of the girls here."

Then I laugh some more. I laugh at their fear and they look like they want to die with shame.

Stupid useless girls.

I am stuck with Anikó as a dental assistant all day and she spends the whole time terrified and handing me the wrong instruments and turning off the light when I ask her to turn it on. I just sigh and tell her to sort herself out. I want to say 'I said turn the light on, not turn me on, goddamn.'

But I figure I have said enough for today.

I get home that night and my arrogant front splinters and falls to the ground. I cry and cry and cry myself to sleep that night. I am an asshole and I fucked it up with Lilla. I try to think how it started going so wrong, who hurt who first. It was probably me. If I had known about her father's death I would have tried to get her help before all her self-destructive behaviour and maybe none of this cheating and hurting and violence would have happened. I wouldn't have bullied her, been so violently possessive; I should have trusted her and she wouldn't have cheated on me. She would have remained devoted and sweet. I am to blame.

And I cry for my parents who died in a car crash when I was at medical school. They were so loving and it would kill them to see how their only child turned out. Successful, handsome and horribly cruel. A sadist who hates women. Maybe if Kiára was alive, it would all have been okay. Yes it would, I would never have got to this stage. They used to be so proud of me and my achievements.

I don't think I cried so much in my life. And I long

for Lilla to be there to comfort me as she was at her best when I needed her, when I was ill and depressed. Even now, after all her cheating I want her there, stroking my hair. I must be a masochist as well as a sadist to put up with all the damage she has done to my heart. We both are. We both hurt each other and get hurt.

I hate myself.

I hate what I have become. Kiára would be so ashamed of me.

And everyone thinks I am an arrogant man who loves himself. They are so wrong.

EMPTINESS

I go to the opera alone. This is not a good idea. It is La Bohème and I can't help but think how I was here in the opera house last with Lilla to see Carmen. I should not be watching Puccini as during the part where Mimi is out in the snow singing her sad aria, I start crying myself thinking I have cast Lilla out in a similar way and I cannot bear to watch the ending where Mimi dies. So I leave and the street is snow swirling despite it being March and it is unseasonably cold. I cannot see between the tears and the snowstorm. I manage to open a taxi door outside the opera house and climb in and cry all the way home. Fuck it; the taxi driver probably won't remember me.

He keeps asking me *am I okay? Is someone ill?*

Yes, I say. *My wife and I threw her out. I need to get her home safe.*

Kata is waiting for me and asks me *what happened? I am early.*

Nothing, nothing, I say.

She hands me a letter. It was in the mailbox. It is from Lilla.

I skim through it and Lilla is telling me she cheated on the one person she loved more than anything. Not just once, but again and again.

'Not because they were better than you, not because I wanted to but because my heart kept telling me to kill any love I had before it left me, before you left me. I don't know why I did it. After that day you told me to leave when we were in Rome, I just began to destroy anything sweet. I wanted to die when I took those pills. I didn't do it to get your attention, I just thought everyone would be better off if I died. My mother, Levente, Natalija but especially you.

I know this time I really destroyed everything

because I felt I was unloveable and it becomes a self-fulfilling prophecy. I wish so much I could go back and do it all right, to start from when I met you. I think about you all the time and I don't want anyone else. I didn't realise what I had until I threw it away and now I am suffering. I was so stupid, so heartless.

I will always love you, István. I know you hurt me at times but it is nothing to what I put you through.

Your Lilla'

I get into the bath with the letter and read it again and cry so much because I have lost her. She has said at the beginning of the letter that when I threw her out, she went back to her mother who told her she wasn't setting foot in her apartment and to go and sell herself or get a job in a strip club as she had more or less sold herself to me.

What a bitch Ágnes is. What a goddamn bitch. Lilla has some money in one of our joint bank accounts and I hope she will be using it until I find her. I will make sure there is always money in there. I have to find her.

She cheated on me, she broke my heart again and again but who the Hell is to say you leave someone because they cheat. Many people do and many people don't. Lilla cheated because she was damaged, not because she loved anyone else.

I know she will have changed her cell phone number. As I try it even before I reach the automated message telling me the phone is no longer in service, I know. Even an email I try to send pings back. She has closed her email account.

She has disappeared without a trace.

I tell Kata and I phone Zsolt as both of them know about the two separate wills I have. After watching La Bohème and seeing Mimi cast into the snow I tell them, "Destroy the will where only the children get my money. It is to go to Lilla and them. I want her to have my money. I love her."

Zsolt says *I must go to my lawyer and make this official if I am sure. If I am sure that Lilla will not hurt me again.*

I am sure, I tell him and I call the lawyer and make an appointment.

I now need to find the ghost of the woman I once searched for. As I searched for Kiára, I now need to find her reincarnation. I need to find Lilla.

REINCARNATION

It is a month later when I see her again. Right after Kiára's birthday in April; I have had no pleading calls, no texts, no begging to come home, just the heartbreaking letter which was so final. I guess she knew she had really betrayed me this time. I am in a restaurant thinking about Kiára and the anniversary of her death and I wish so hard she would just walk in and sit down opposite me, just for one night. *Just one night for her to return to earth and be with me.*

All through the restaurant there seem to be couples, happy couples and my heart burns. I am alone and all I want is Kiára to come back to me. As I am thinking this, a glamorous woman arrives with a much older man and they head to the back of the restaurant, an escort girl no doubt so I am not really looking at them. I am lost in my Kiára fantasy, but when she turns to remove her coat, I see her face. It is Lilla. So she has finally been honest and admitted she needs to charge for her services. She sees me and looks sadly over at the table, longing to speak but she knows I know what she is doing. The dental surgery said she could go back anytime but I guess she couldn't face me. She quit after I threw her out of my apartment.

Again as I had tried to find her, I called her cold-hearted mother who told me she threw her out the second she arrived on her doorstep and then hung up the phone. So the letter is true, her mother is as bad as she says. I threw her out because of what she did but her mother? I am lost for words by this Ágnes and her callous treatment of her daughter. For what? Because she married me and had my child. No wonder Lilla is so damaged, so unable to form normal relationships. I walked the streets of the downtown especially on a Sunday feeling like I wasn't or more like I am not over her. I just wanted to see her as crazy as it would sound to other people who would tell me I was mad; *hasn't this girl hurt you enough?* I didn't have the numbers of any of her friends but knowing Lilla now, she will not ask for help. I even went into some notorious strip bars and show Lilla's photo asking does she work there. I have no luck.

So to see her appear in the restaurant through some twist of fate just as I am thinking about my long lost love is a shock but I am more sad than angry when I realise Lilla is selling her body. It leaves me with such emptiness. She never needed to do that. Ever. She cheated on me, but why the Hell did she turn into a call girl? I want to go over there and take her back now but I am too proud when I think about her cheating. *In my bed.* I want to forgive her but my pride is stopping me going over and just taking her out of the restaurant, away from this man and back to my apartment.

I leave the restaurant right after them as I have to see where they are going and I will follow in a taxi and talk to her when she leaves this sleazy man's hotel room. Even if I have to sit there all night. She is waiting for me outside in the cold; Lilla the ice princess. The man is sitting impatient in his sleek silver car looking annoyed. He looks about 70.

"Go away, Lilla, go and earn your money," I say and start to walk along the street. My pride burns and I can't say what I need to say.

"Tell me, István. Please tell me there is still a chance," she says. "I miss you, I miss my son, I miss Natalija."

I turn back to look at her but I cannot speak. There are no words I can say now. I want to but I can't.

I leave her standing on Andrássy Út in her fur coat, her diamonds, all that remains of us. Beautiful and damaged Lilla.

"I love you..." she says.

I thought that my heart closed for good when she betrayed me the last time. I think of the pain and rage of finding her cheating in my bed and I want to beat her all over again.

Yet I have been looking for her so sadly all over the city, longing to see her again.

I say nothing and I turn and walk away. What can I say? I could say 'I don't love you and I never did,' but even that seems beyond me to be so cruel because she does love me and I would be lying to myself to say that. Somewhere in my closed heart the love still burns and will not stop. Her cheating and crazy behaviour aside, there is a love between us which burns so deep, which is why she couldn't face me in work.

I could have faced her in the clinical setting of the dental surgery, not because I had no feelings left for her, more that I have stuffed my love into such a dark chasm in my soul I feel it will never be released again. The embers would just smoulder on in my heart. If she had carried on working at the surgery, it would be all the same to me. I am in a different world when I am working; I forget everything and concentrate on dentistry.

This meeting has stirred me up but I do nothing. The words are there and I am too proud to tell her *I still want her, that I have been trying to find her so desperately. I want her in my bed and in my life.* I want to fuck her and take her home forever but I cannot say anything. She has not got my restraint. She chases me down the street and tells me *she wants to come home, please let me come home and sleep in the spare room. I will do anything, anything and I miss Natalija and Levente and I love you. I love you so much.* She falls to the floor weeping at my feet and everyone walking past in the night chill stares at us.

God, how many times have we been here?

She clings to my knees and says, "Don't leave me, don't leave me."

And my heart begins to crack and splinter and I can feel it stabbing away in my chest as well as something deep and primal stirring within; *she is mine. No one else can have her.* I need to fight and take her back from all these men who are fucking her. I am not going to lose her to all these losers. She is my wife and suddenly I want to kill this man and all the others who want to fuck her for money.

I go up to the man in the silver car, Lilla's client and knock on his window. "How much does she owe you?" I ask.

He opens the window. "What?" He looks at me like I am crazy.

"She's my wife; I need to take her home. How much do I have to give you?"

"300 euros plus the dinner, little whore tricked me. Are you her pimp?" he says.

I lean in and grab him by the throat. "I am her husband, you filthy German fuck. She is my wife. She is not a whore. She is just a girl, a damaged teenage girl, you sick son of a bitch."

Silver hair in his silver car coughs and chokes and gasps for air as I pull the notes from my wallet and drop them through his window.

I go back to Lilla who is kneeling on the cold street, watching me and I gently pick her up, "Come on baby, come on, we'll just go home now."

She has stopped crying and I carry her into my taxi and take her home. *God, Lilla when did you last eat something? You weigh nothing.* She doesn't speak, just rests her face against me. The taxi driver who saw all this street theatre and probably heard it all too says very little apart from, "Still cold for this time of year. Still cold. It's not right. It should be warm in April."

"Yes," I say. *Cruel and cold for April.* I press my face into Lilla's fur coat and against her cheek

We say nothing to each other in the taxi.

I curse my weakness. I feel aroused and I hate myself. I want to rip off her clothes and feel that silken body next to me.

Natalija lets herself be embraced and although I can see she is happy to see Lilla, she is not overjoyed. No longer will she look at her adoringly. She accepts her presence but has distanced herself from the girl she once thought was her mother. She knows Lilla isn't her mother now.

She disappears back into her room and shuts the door.

Lilla goes to see Levente as Kata is leaving. "Nice to see you Lilla, he is sleeping now."

Kata has seen the worst of Lilla. She has taken care of our son since July and she still doesn't have a bad word to say to her, this lovely lady, unlike the bitches in the dental surgery.

I can't imagine for one minute she goes home and says to her husband 'that family I work for; they are so fucked up.' She probably has no judgement of any of us.

I go into the kitchen. I need a cup of coffee.

Lilla paws at my arm. "Tell me my love, is there anything I can do. Is there any way for us?" she looks at me with her gorgeous face but that heart of a demon.

'Tell her you love her,' my heart is saying but instead I tell her, "No, sweetheart. It is dead. We are well and truly over. It was nice of you to write to me." But I know she wouldn't be here if we were over. I am lying and she knows. I am struggling to control my emotions.

"You still want me. I know you do. You just paid that man and brought me home." she tries to kiss me and I push her away.

"I don't want a goddamn part of you now, Lilla. But I am not having my wife doing that and someone seeing you. I have my pride and yes, I did feel pity but that's all. You must have slept with hundreds of men. God knows what diseases you have. Like you said, you sleep in the spare room from now on."

"I did it because you threw me out, because my mother threw me out. I did it because I had no choice. And I have no diseases; I had myself tested, I always had safe sex. I only worked two nights a week for the last month. I was going to stop as soon as I found work in a hotel."

"You could still work in the dental surgery, they would still want you there. You chose to leave," I tell her. *Miss Safe Sex. God, how many times have I heard that one. Oh, don't worry you screwed the whole city, because you used condoms.*

"Because I only loved you. István, I only loved you," she says. "To see you every day and not be with you hurts." She is honest when she says this. If she didn't care she could have carried on with her receptionist job, flirting with young men. She could have hurt me or tried to.

"You don't have a heart to hurt. In my bed, Lilla. After everything you put me through, all the broken promises and the final insult to find you like that, getting well and truly laid in my bed," I tell her. "And I never thought I would ever see you again, Lilla. I thought I had lost you." I bite my lips to stop myself from crying.

"Please let me stay. Please let me. I will do anything. I will take the job back in the surgery," she falls to her knees her hands clasped in prayer. "I promise I will take care of the son you wanted so much. I swear I will never cheat. You are so handsome and I fucked up so badly. You are the best looking man I could ever be with, my darling husband. And I know why you would be sad this time of year, Kiára's birthday and her anniversary. I am so sorry. I fucked everything up."

God, you are such a manipulative bitch. You have such a whore's touch, you know exactly how to play me, I think as she starts to run her hands along my legs. *Goddamn Lilla. God, stop before I lose control.* I am angry. With myself and with her. I still want her. I want her now, on the floor, savage and wild, hair pulling, claws scratching, biting, *Oh God help me I want her.*

Lilla, I think I love you. I never stopped loving you however much you cheated.

I lift her up and gently put her in the spare room, and she begs me to hurt her. "Beat me, like you did before, hurt me," she says crying. But I can't, I just can't bring myself to do it. I hate myself for beating her like that just as I hate myself for cheating on her and for hurting that drunk American girl. All these things make me a horrible man. I am a sadist.

"I can't. I can't beat you," I tell her.

"Why? I deserve it," she says looking up at me.

"Because I fucking love you, Lilla. Haven't you worked that one out yet? Why would I take you back after everything you did? You had everything with me and you threw it all away and I thought I would never ever find you again," I say.

And I realise despite all her cheating, I never stopped loving her. I was cruel too. I should have got her help instead of getting angry and throwing her out in Rome, instead of saying cruel things, beating her, hurting her. She is a damaged young girl.

I remembered the other day the Italian dresses I bought in the airport in Rome. I go to fetch them from the wardrobe where they have been hanging waiting for her since January. I give them to her now. "These were bought in Rome, as I was leaving," I say as she touches the beautiful cloth.

"You see, Lilla. Even when you drove me crazy, I never ever stopped thinking about you."

I hear her crying as she looks at the dresses and I close the door.

I don't want her to think she can just climb right back into my bed. I want to keep her at a distance. I should have locked the door because when I am asleep she snakes into my bed, this serpent and slides her soft hands along my back and kisses my neck. If I really didn't want her to come in I would have locked the door as I knew she couldn't sleep in the spare room, knew she would slither into my bed at some point tonight. Maybe this is what I wanted.

My body is weak. I am a weak man. I try to ignore it but I can't. I turn over and bury my face in her neck and kiss her and taste that sweet honey skin and slide on top of her. And I want to hurt her as I am so angry but I have to stop this hurting. I could kill her at times but what does that make me, whatever she has done? But I taste the salt from my tears as I kiss her and she holds me and I cry into her face, "Lilla, my Lilla what did we do to each other?" I bite her shoulder but gently, I can't hurt her tonight.

"It's okay, István. I will make it okay." And her soft gentle hands stroke my hair and face until we fall asleep wrapped so tightly I can hardly breathe.

After this, I can't pretend. I hate and love this demon who arouses me but I have to stop resisting and I let her stay with me each night. I am sleeping with the Devil. I have sold my black soul for one which is burned to a cinder. But each night the passion is more hate for me. The love is there but it comes out in violent passion and hate. I never thought I could do this. But I do not want to sleep alone. A man has physical needs and she does all that. The contrast to her 17 year old innocent naive loving is like a lifetime. Well I guess she has had a lifetime of lovers in the last couple of years. She tells me she loves me in my ear every night. But try as I can, I cannot say it back.

Because I love her even though I didn't think I ever did but it is now hidden so deep inside my heart I cannot reach it. I can feel the words inside sticking into me like needles but I just cannot bring myself to say it to her.

But when she is asleep, I admit what has been there since I met her and I stroke her soft skin and think, 'I love you'. I can close my eyes and love my dream; that I am with Kiára and not Lilla. Physically, she is perfect but in the morning the dream is not the same.

She is here for my April sadness, she even remembered without me saying anything and when I return from work that evening she is holding Levente and she has bought me an expensive watch, with her sex money no doubt. The sooner I get her back into her pure white dental reception outfit, the better. I do not want a watch. I have an expensive watch but I don't want to hurt her feelings, so I take off my watch and put on hers. She has put some flowers on the kitchen table and she holds me to her tightly as I sit there as the tears flow down my face for my lost love and my reincarnated new one. She doesn't say anything and neither do I. The skin between the worlds is so fragile and I feel that when my eyes are shut that she is Kiára that evening. More than I ever felt, she is my dead love come back to earth to comfort me. "Kiára I miss you so much," I say.

And she says into my hair, "I am here, I am here for you."

She has come back to me, my love.

I even have started calling her Kiára as I did when

I first met her but she doesn't correct me, or get angry. She understands. She shows me a medical print out from the doctor to show she is clear of all STDs. She wants to prove to me she is no longer a cheat and a liar.

Lilla who finally learned to love.

Natalija is old enough to realise how much Lilla hurt me but she accepts Lilla as someone who takes care of her. She doesn't ask her to play. She says *she is beyond games, the ice is waiting.*

She is disappearing into her own world, Natalija. A world of ice and silver blades. She has my drive, my ambition; she will be a champion ice skater. Lilla has damaged her too, not deliberately just through her reckless, careless behaviour.

But it is not Lilla's fault, I remind myself. *You hurt her too. Everyone in her life hurt her.*

Levente will be too young to remember how Lilla neglected him and hated him. He is only 9 months old but he has always had enough love and attention from me and the au pair.

She did what I suggested and returned to work in the dental surgery as receptionist but only part-time.

The love that I don't want to admit still lies there in my shattered heart. Hopelessly distorted, misshapen and hidden too deep to grasp, but it is a love all the same.

And there is no denying it; I wished for my dead love to return that night in the restaurant and Lilla walked in and she is a different Lilla. I see more traces of my lost love of my life reincarnated but maybe it is wishful thinking. I hate to sleep alone. Those lonely years after losing Kiára were the bleakest I have experienced. The loss of her warm body next to me was what I found hardest to live without. I don't have to starve, I am not betraying her by being with someone else. I am keeping her memory alive with the closest living soul I could hope to find, if only she had more smouldering depth, but then would Kiára have been any different at Lilla's age?

We both hurt each other and we both cheated and broke each other and our hearts are smashed to pieces. As I curl up next to Lilla I think, who else would we be with? We did so much damage.

Who else would tolerate such extremes? Such cruelty with the lying and the cheating, the pushing each other to the limits of pain physically and mentally?

Most people would be several countries apart by now.

But we are not most people. And through all that fire of hatred and anger and jealous passion, burned a slow love so intense it obliterated everything in its path.

INFINITY

I look through the bedroom window at the lights shining in the darkness where other people are existing in each apartment. I wonder if anyone really loves or whether they are living lies too. It is midnight and mid-summer and the world seems to have lost its sharp edges but also its excitement and danger. For me anyway.

I still view these beautiful lights in the darkness, like the chain bridge at night or the fairytale castle, which never lose their midnight magic no matter how often you drive past but they are only an illusion as in the morning their loveliness is gone, the lights extinguished. Once I thought Lilla was like that; a beautiful light dazzling in the black sky, a princess made of crystal who belonged in an amber palace. Only now I know she was a young careless girl when I met her. She was just a child.

I think back to the time I wanted to crash the car and kill both of us with flames of jealousy and passion, like lovers burning together in a volcano with their flesh melting into one. I think about how I beat her cruelly when I caught her cheating in my own bed, my kingdom and I feel such guilt.

It seems like a long time ago now. We have given up on hating each other.

When I look at her in the flickering candlelight of our bedroom, I see my real love brought back to life in this 21 year old. She looks like her more than ever and in the half-light when I close my eyes and inhale her perfume, I try to love with my dark heart. It is only the memory of Kiára I really love. *My love, my life, my everything.* This girl is only a ghost of her, but at night she becomes real enough for me to believe it is her. God knows how I didn't divorce this girl who burnt through my layers of skin like a volcano. I didn't want anyone to say, 'I told you so, I told you the age gap was too much.'

And maybe I had just gone through too much to let her go. I never want to let her go. Whatever she did wrong, however she slashed me to pieces with her careless heart. We loved, we hurt and we smashed up and destroyed the amber palace between us.

I am dulled by these meds as I am on a high dose to ensure I do not have any more episodes. I find the anger has gone but the good emotions have levelled into something monotonous, which is why until I was 42 even when I knew I needed medication I always resisted it. It is a world without swirling bright colours as though everything is painted in soft watercolour. Gentle, but lacking the excitement I crave.

Even now when Lilla hasn't cheated for the year and two months she has been home and her childish moods are over, I am empty. I am her husband and I have control; I have won in the end but the victory feels hollow. I haven't felt like King István for a long time so to call Levente 'heir to the throne' sounds strange now. He is just a lovely carbon copy of me but he is not immortal. Lilla adores him, surprising me as I didn't think she ever would.

Lilla is not the love of my life; she is the spirit and body of the woman who was. I was and still am existing on a fabric of lies. I tried to hunt down the impossible which only lived in the heart of one person. I could have searched the world and never found it. My mistake was believing in its existence and it did explode like a volcano and we are both damaged from the falling rocks and molten lava of hateful emotions. We should have stayed apart, my shrink was right. I should never have met her that frozen beautiful day in January when the sun lit up what I thought was my dream come true, my reincarnated Kiára. I should not have gone looking for ghosts.

It could have destroyed both of us. But as I hold what I wanted so badly, I am glad I searched and found the ghost I needed or I would still be alone and grieving.

I worry so much about Lilla's health; I try to look after her. Her liver was damaged after her overdose that time and she was in danger of needing a transplant. She has recovered but I am taking care of her like the delicate crystal I once saw her as. At times I cry into her hair when she sleeps when I think back to how cruel and possessive I was. I hold her at night and I pray her liver will regenerate as the specialist is hoping for. I lost her so many times I could not bear to lose her again. It would kill me. As again, I would feel responsible like I did with Kiára.

But she has no fire, no volcano within her now and I wonder if I needed strife and arguments and passion to survive, to keep me burning. Lilla is like a fire gone out. But there is no denying fire and hate are exhausting and no good for the bipolar condition. I need her so badly, more than I have ever needed anyone. We go out together as a family, the four of us and people admire our beauty and the lovely children. There is no volcanic passion until the night when she sticks her claws in my back only this time she tells me she loves me but I cannot say it back because I am lost and with the ghost of my only real love.

She brings Levente into the surgery to show off, now 2 years old; all black corkscrew curls and dark eyes and a lovely smile. The women are jealous of Lilla with her beauty and her adorable little boy. They don't know the darkness which has dominated our relationship.

"A clone of István," she says happily lifting my

gorgeous son in the air. I find her adoration of me touching, after so much hatred. I hope Levente doesn't inherit my personality. I hope he never turns vicious like I did, lashing out at the women who admire his good looks. I am not a good man; I am cruel and sadistic and controlling. When I was angry I hoped he would grow up just like me. Now I want the opposite.

The men are envious as Lilla is more beautiful and sensual at 21 than she was when I met her and I hear the other male dentists say to each other, "God, what I wouldn't do to have her in my bed. He is a lucky guy, that István. He gets everything he wants."

There is not a chance Lilla will be in their beds. Finally she is the girl I wanted. She is devoted to me, to Natalija and our son. *No one will take her from me again.*

Losing someone she adored shocked her into growing up; she never loved me as much as when I threw her out those times. She was so cool and calm when I first met her and she was heartless and careless with my love. I am grateful to have her, to have finally possessed her but I am exhausted with the fight. It nearly broke my life and not just my heart.

We broke each other again and again; we made each other suffer and splinter and go crazy with our twisted and damaged love. No one knows the suffering we inflicted on each other.

When Lilla is out I stare obsessively at Kiára's photos. The ones I framed are on the living room wall and for Lilla, I have placed her there too. The photos could almost be of the same beautiful woman, only one is slightly older. There are two of great contrasts as though they are splits of one personality; the first is Lilla on her wedding day in her glistening white snow queen outfit, an ice princess with a heart just as frozen. The other is of Kiára in burning red, smouldering with vitality although there is a sadness in her dark eyes; a look which betrays her pain within. A heart which loved too much and eventually failed.

Tomorrow and the day after tomorrow and all of my days stretch into infinity and we exist without the volcanic passion, without the burning love I still crave but which is so dangerous. And into infinity and beyond is my love for Kiára.

'Kiára I write this for you. I hope you can forgive me for what I did, for the man I turned into. You made me a better man for the short time I was with you. I think I have found you again in this young girl but I should not have let you out of my sight because I messed up. I longed for you, I searched for you and when I found your spirit and your body in Lilla, all I did was control and hold you so tightly and imprison you and be cruel and I can't take it back. And now I can love only if I hide it. Hidden in the deep chasm which exists between fantasy and reality in my mind is the feeling that the Lilla who is you could break me again. She could leave again. I don't want to give a voice to this fear in case I make it real. But the more I see how Lilla has changed in the last year or so I know she is slowly becoming you, my long lost love.'

Some people would say that this is no way to live but it is the only way I can exist; between the desolation of loneliness and the jagged rocks of our twisted, once treacherous love, I have chosen this path. The chance I had to turn around and take a safe road has long since passed. I wonder what would have happened if I had crashed the car that night when I was crying and she was pleading with me to stop. But I loved her so desperately then and now I realise she would not have been worth dying for. This princess was only an illusion. She would always fall short of the love of my life. I would never have thought that this delicate young girl was stronger than me. She smashed my heart to fragments. Many times. Until it remained broken and although I can still love my Lilla, I can only whisper it in the darkness as she sleeps as it is so locked away in my blackened soul.

You have stopped haunting me, Kiára so I believe you are at peace now. I feel you have finally possessed this sweet girl who has reverted back to the gentle loving Lilla I first met. Maybe all that fighting, all that hatred between us was really you, Kiára as you possessed Lilla with your volcanic passion. Maybe you were still angry with me for not saving your life.

But I have started to rebuild the amber palace for my ice princess. I am slowly finding the fragments of the beautiful amber and moulding them together until it is done. She is my dead love brought back to life. I know it.

My one love of my life. Will always be. Into infinity.

Now, as her reincarnated soul sleeps angelic next to me, I can lie to myself best of all.

I whisper, "Kiára, I love you." And it is real enough for me.